COLD BLOODED

A GIA SANTELLA CRIME THRILLER
BOOK 10

KRISTI BELCAMINO

LIQUID MIND PUBLISHING

Huge thanks to Hilary Hafeken, Tara Stapledon, Lu Curtis, Karen Davis, Kate Carroll, Margaret Souayah, and John Bychowski for helping polish this book for publication!

Liquid Mind Publishing
This is a work of fiction. All characters, names, places and events are the product of the author's imagination or used fictitiously.

GIA SANTELLA CRIME THRILLER SERIES

Enjoying the Gia Santella series? Scan below to order more books today!

Vendetta

Vigilante

Vengeance

Black Widow

Day of the Dead

Border Line

Night Fall

Stone Cold

Cold as Death

Cold Blooded

Dark Shadows

Dark Vengeance

Dark Justice

Deadly Justice

Deadly Lies

PROLOGUE

THE ICY OCEAN AIR WHIPS MY HAIR BACK, AND I FRANTICALLY brush it aside so I can see in front of me as the large boat I'm steering slices through the choppy water.

The darkness seems impenetrable and goes on forever. The horizon is only a slightly lighter black. I check the compass. I'm heading in the right direction.

But it's taking too long.

The clock is ticking.

I'm going to be too late.

And I'm going to lose everything.

I tamp down the dread and anxiety and fear. I concentrate on the rage. My fury will fuel me, whereas my worry will knock my legs out from under me if I let it gain the upper hand.

What I don't think about is people I love dying horrific deaths.

I only think about the revenge I'm going to wreak upon every last person who put me in this situation.

If I survive this, they will wish they were dead when I show up.

I vow this. I will avenge the pain they caused me and my

loved ones if it's the last thing I do. This determination helps me not to think about what I am heading toward.

Again, it's taking too long. Much too long.

I need to find them. Now.

The boat is going as fast as it can go and I can feel the vibration throughout my body.

But it's not fast enough.

Then in the dark I see something. A shape, still indistinct on the horizon, but a lighter black then the rest. It *has* to be them. It *has* to.

Thank God.

I'm coming. I'm coming. I'm coming.

I chant the words to myself. Or maybe it's just in my head.

All moisture has been wicked from my mouth and despite the thrum of the engine noise, I can hear my heartbeat in my ears. My entire body feels electric. With fear. With dread.

I turn my head to see the dark shape even better when there is a terrific explosion.

The night sky is filled with an orange-white inferno that is nearly blinding.

The horrific boom of the blast reverberates across the water.

It drowns out my screams.

I'm too late.

San Diego

I CAN SMELL the ocean from my secluded backyard. We have high stone walls for privacy that are bordered with tropical plants. The entire patio is surrounded by plants. A gurgling fountain in the corner and soft Afro-Cuban music filtering out hidden speakers provides a soothing soundtrack. Bougainvillea flowers scent the whole back yard.

I'm sprawled on the cushioned chaise lounge end of the patio furniture sipping a mojito and reading Fiore Dei Liberi's "Armizare." Django is at my feet on the sandstone patio, his head on his paws, one eye watching me like a sentry.

Nico took Rosalie to the park down the street to give me some time to myself.

It's the anniversary of Bobby's murder.

If I close my eyes I'm back in that hotel courtyard in Positano, Italy, searching the dead bodies for the man I love. I can see my best friend Dante holding onto his husband of mere hours, willing him to live. But Matt also died. Just not right away.

The killer was after me. I have to live with that forever. It's not easy.

I avenged Bobby and Matt's deaths. But of course, that's never enough. It doesn't bring back those you love.

I've set down my book and I'm remembering Bobby. How one moonlit night in Positano we got it right. We cut through all the bullshit and got down to the essence—pure love. I'm so grateful we had that moment before he was taken away from me.

For years, I thought I was incapable of loving again.

Until Nico.

As the birds sing and chirp around me in this idyllic back yard, I count my blessings. I finally have what I've always yearned for—a family. A normal life.

Nico's job under his Witness Protection program is a financial analyst. He gets up every day, goes to his office at one corner of the house and works under his new name, Damien Costa. I tease him that his fake name sounds more Italian than Mexican. He does not find that funny.

And I spend my days as a mom. I get up and pack a lunch for

Rosalie and make her breakfast, which is usually cereal or biscotti or toast. Nico likes to walk her to the bus stop, so he takes a break to do that.

Then he goes back to his office and works. I always take Django for a long walk on the beach and then come home and lay in the sun on the patio and read. At least that's the pattern I've established since I moved here six months ago. I've got a killer tan, now.

Nico takes a late lunch and we always eat together and then go to our big, airy bedroom and make love. The bedroom has huge French doors that open up to the patio. The only thing in the bedroom is our huge bed with white bedding. It's my sanctuary.

In the afternoon, Nico takes a break to meet Rosalie at the bus stop while I make her a snack.

I supervise her homework at the kitchen counter and then she gets some TV time while Nico and I have a drink on the patio. Then, close to eight, Nico makes us dinner. Mostly because I'm a shit cook and he has mad skills in the kitchen.

It is a dream life.

We are secluded from the world and we love it.

Today, Saturday, is the day Nico spends most of the day with Rosalie doing something fun.

It's the one day he really gets out of the house.

I used to worry someone would recognize him. But he looks so different from his old life as a cartel leader. He's leaner and tanner and has let his hair go silver and grow long on the sides. He has a goatee now, too.

He also wears dark sunglasses whenever he leaves the house.

I don't really worry as much anymore, but I have to admit I always breathe a big sigh of relief when he is back home again.

I glance at the clock. He and Rosalie probably won't be home for another hour or two. He promised her ice cream down at the beach after the park.

I pad in bare feet back into the house and make another mojito. My cell phone is on the counter. I pick it up. It's time to call Dante. I've been putting it off for the last hour.

I know he no longer blames me for Matt's death, but I still blame myself.

Back on the patio, I drink half my mojito before I dial.

He picks up but doesn't speak.

"I love you, Dante."

He exhales loudly. "I love you, too, Gia."

"What are you doing?" He sounds like he just woke up when I called and I'm right.

"In bed."

"Oh."

"You?"

"On my second mojito."

"It's just now noon," he says.

"Yep," I say.

"Hold on."

"Okay."

I wait and wait. And then he gets back on.

"Matched you," he says.

"Oh, yeah?"

"I just pounded two glasses of Chivas Regal."

"And you didn't barf?"

"Haha."

"What's that sound?" I ask.

"Rain."

"Oh, my God," I say. "I don't miss that at all. It's fucking perfect weather down here every goddamn day. I'm not kidding."

"I hate the rain," Dante says. "I hate everything right now, Gia."

"Mmm," I say. I don't tell him that the manager at the restaurant he owns called me yesterday because Dante hasn't been coming to work. And when he went to check on him, he found him in bed.

"Dante, how many days have you been in bed?"

"What?"

"How many?"

"Six, maybe seven."

"That's fucked up. Come down here."

"I'm never going to find anyone like Matt. Ever."

"That's not true," I say. "I thought the same thing and then I met Nico."

"That's not going to happen to me."

"You're right," I say. "Because you are only dating Boy Toys."

"So?"

"Duh," I say. "They're not marriage material, now are they?"

He is quiet.

"Dante?"

"Yeah."

"But seriously, I think you are afraid to date anyone in your league. You need to find a successful business man like yourself. But you keep dating these Fuck Boys. Because I think deep down inside you don't want to get serious again because you're afraid."

"Okay, fucking Freud, can we change the subject already?"

"Only if you agree to get your ass down here."

"I can't. I have two restaurants to run."

"I call bullshit. You have a team in place to run everything while you are gone."

"Maybe."

"Please come down here. It's heavenly."

"I can't."

"There's a ticket waiting for you at the Oakland airport. Your flight leaves at eight. I'll pick you up at the airport. See you tonight."

I hang up. And smile imagining him scrambling to get packed.

I refuse to imagine him staying in bed.

1

Nico makes crab and shrimp enchiladas for dinner and we eat out on the patio.

"You need to make these again this week when Dante's here," I say, stuffing a huge bite in my mouth. "These are the best thing I ever tasted."

"Gia's right," Rosalie says, shuffling a forkful of food in her mouth. "Yum, Daddy!"

Nico beams. And lifts his wine glass. "You two are my motivation to make beautiful and delicious food. You know what the main ingredient is, right?" he says.

Rosalie rolls her eyes, but answers on cue: "Love."

"That's right, my darling," he says.

We smile at each other over the candles. The sun has just set. I'm going to leave for the airport as soon as we are done, so I'm only sipping my one glass of wine.

"Do you think he'll be there?" Rosalie asks, reading my mind.

I smile. "I do. I would be surprised if he didn't come. But with Dante you never know."

"Is he really sad right now?" she asks.

"Yes. It's the anniversary of the day his husband died."

I never mince words with Rosalie. The child has seen people she loved murdered in front of her more than once. She is wise and knowing in ways that break my heart.

"That's why I'm going to learn karate," she says and makes a chopping motion with her hand.

Nico gives me an alarmed look.

I look down.

"What is this you are speaking about, my dear?" he asks Rosalie, but his black eyes are boring into mine.

"Gia says I should take some martial arts classes so I can protect myself," Rosalie says. Then as if she senses the tension she looks back and forth from me to Nico.

I push back my chair.

"I should head to the airport now."

I don't meet Nico's eyes.

But he doesn't let it go.

"Gia says you should learn karate?"

She frowns. "I don't know if she called it karate, but some type of martial arts. Yes."

I am almost home free. I kiss Rosalie on the top of the head and start to walk by Nico but he reaches for my wrist. I stop.

"Maybe we can talk about the martial arts thing later?"

"Sure, Nico."

As I drive to the airport I try to come up with an argument against Nico's objections to Rosalie taking martial arts classes. I pretty much know what he is going to say already.

One of the reasons he agreed to go into Witness Protection was so he could give Rosalie a normal life. In his view, teaching her how to fight or even defend herself is not what "normal" little girls do.

But I disagree. I lived a fairly normal childhood and took

martial arts classes. Granted, it wasn't until I was older and picked on in high school, but still.

The thing that Nico and I will never see eye-to-eye about is that it truly is impossible for Rosalie to have a so-called normal childhood. She's seen more violence and murder than most people have in a life time. She's also the daughter of a man who will always have a hit on his head. She needs to know how to defend herself.

See, martial arts are just the tip of the iceberg. I intend to teach her *gladiatura moderna*–the Italian form of martial arts involving weapons, such as swords and daggers. And then I'll teach her to shoot.

This girl is not going out in the real world without the ability to defend herself.

If Nico thinks I'm going to back down on this he has another thing coming.

2

Dante is waiting out at the curb for me to pick him up.

For a guy who spent the last week in bed depressed, he looks amazing. Women are checking him out as they walk past.

He has no clue.

He never has.

With his black silky hair swept back, bronze skin and blindingly white smile, he's an Italian-American hunk. He has on a loose white linen top unbuttoned and I can see his shiny gold Italian cornetto and hand—the horn and the hand are good luck. They both protect you against the evil eye, the malocchio.

He has on loose black linen pants rolled up and Gucci loafers.

Dante is my fashion idol. Whenever I need to dress up outside of leather pants and a band T-shirt, he hooks me up.

But I have to say my worn in uniform of leather pants has been neglected since I've moved to San Diego. I have been living in bikinis and loose black sundresses with flip-flops. It's been a nice change.

I pull up in my Lincoln Navigator with Cardi B. blaring. Everyone looks. I don't give a fuck.

I'm pumped. I'm excited to see my best friend.

And I'm going to make sure he has a good time down here. Starting now.

He looks over and sees me and grins.

I park illegally and hop out, running over to give him a huge bear hug.

"Gia!" He picks me up and swings me around. I love this man.

He laughs as I lead him by the hand to the car. He's only got a small leather duffel bag so he hops in and throws it in the back seat.

"I think that's the lightest I've ever seen you travel in all the years we've been friends, Dante," I say. "Usually you have an entire suitcase just for your shoes."

He shakes his head. "Well, I usually have more than twenty minutes to pack for a trip."

"True," I say as I navigate airport traffic to get on the freeway. "But aren't you going to have withdrawals?"

"I brought four outfits identical to what I have on, some swim shorts, and some sandals. What else do I need? This is a beach vacation, right?"

I shrug, but then smile at him. "You've got all your bases covered with that outfit. You can roll up the pants for casual and wear them as is for fancy. But then again, Dante, you'd make a white tee-shirt and cut off shorts look stylish and elegant."

"Probably," he says.

I slug his shoulder.

He has his window down and his arm hanging out.

"It's like forty degrees warmer here," he says.

"Damn right."

Then I turn and am on the road bordering the ocean.

"You live on the beach?" he says.

"I wish," I say and pull over to the side of the road where

there is a wide shoulder and a scenic overlook bench. "Witness protection picked our house."

"Oh, yeah, I almost forgot," he said.

"We're going to get out here for a second," I say. I reach into the back seat and get out my little picnic basket.

Dante gets out and stretches and I pat the bench.

"Have a seat."

Inside the picnic basket is a bottle of Champagne and two flutes.

I pop the cork, pour two glasses and hand one to Dante.

He takes it without comment.

"To Bobby and Matt," I say.

I know I should say more, but that's all I have. It's going to have to be enough.

"To Bobby and Matt," Dante says and raises his glass to mine. They clink and we both take a sip in silence.

We are both staring out at the sea. The moon is not full but light enough to make the ocean before us sparkle. I feel both grief and peace. Two emotions that shouldn't be felt at the same time.

I let Dante decide when it's time to leave. After sitting there for about ten minutes in silence, he stands. "I'm hungry."

"I can do something about that," I say.

We pile back in the Lincoln and pull into my garage ten minutes later.

When we walk in the house, Rosalie jumps out from behind the kitchen counter and shouts, "Surprise!"

Nico is behind the counter at the stove and shouts, "Here he is!"

Django loses his fucking mind and starts making some weird yipping noise that sounds like he's a little girl screaming and rolling her "Rs" at the same time. He's wriggling all over and winding himself around Dante's body like a cat. The only thing keeping him from jumping up and putting his paws on Dante's shoulders is some form of restraint from the past two years of training. Finally, he gives up and has his paws on Dante's shoulders and is licking his face.

"Django!" I scold in a gentle tone and he drops to the ground and continues his wriggling. So cute.

Then Dante is kneeling and hugging Rosalie, who is squealing with delight.

I meet Nico's eyes.

Seeing Rosalie like this will never get old.

Her joy is contagious.

Nico scoops something out onto a plate and sets it on the counter.

"Hungry?"

Dante shakes his head. "You know it."

"It's nothing much," Nico says. "Just some chilaquiles."

It's one of his specialties that he whips up at all hours—it's a cheesy chips mix that is to die for.

"Got more?" I say and pull up a bar stool at the counter next to Dante.

"For you, my love? Always."

And then I'm digging in, as well.

Soon, Rosalie is at the bar beside us eating her own plate.

"Can we play poker before bed?" Rosalie asks.

I cringe. It's my fault but I made the kid a card shark. She plays a mean hand of poker.

I put my arm around her. "Not tonight. Dante is probably tired. Why don't you go get ready for bed and your dad can tuck you in? Dante and I are going to have a glass of wine and then go to bed, too."

"Okay," she says. Then she turns. "I can make Django sleep with you tonight if you want."

"Wow, thanks, Rosie," Dante says. "Why don't we let Django

decide?"

"Okay." As Rosalie leaves Django gives Dante one last look and follows her. Rosalie is Django's girl. His job in life is to protect her. Thank God.

"Sorry," she says.

"No problem. He's better off with you anyway since you don't snore like a chainsaw."

She bursts into giggles and rounds the corner.

After Nico and Rosalie disappear, I pour us wine and lead Dante out to the patio.

"This is my favorite spot," I say. "I'm out here as much as I can be."

We sit in silence for a few seconds, sipping our wine. The only sound is the trickle of the fountain. In the distance, I can hear the crashing of ocean waves. It is only late at night, when the rest of the world is quiet that I can sometimes hear the ocean. It makes my heart sing.

But then I hear some music and giggling.

Dante lifts an eyebrow.

Over our twelve-foot stone wall on one side is a single mother named Gloria.

I've never met her. Her daughter, Julia, goes to the bus stop with Rosalie.

The two girls are becoming friends. Julia has been over a few times for playdates.

Nico and I prefer that for now. It just feels safer to have Rosalie's friends over here than to have her go to someone else's house.

Nico says the mother is very nice and good company while they wait for the bus.

I smile wondering if the mom has a date over tonight. Good for her. It would be tough to be a single mother. No doubt.

Dante yawns.

"I'll show you your room," I say, standing up.

3

IN THE MORNING, DANTE SLEEPS IN LATE, WHICH MAKES ME wonder if he stayed up late the night before in his room. I worry he was having a tough time.

But when he emerges, he's smiling.

He stretches and says, "That's the best night sleep I've had in months. I had the window open all night and there was this ocean breeze and I could hear the waves. Good God, Gia. No wonder you won't come home."

"Right?" I say. Rosalie and I are at the bar in the kitchen drawing.

Nico is in his office.

Rosalie hops up when Dante walks in.

"Want coffee?"

"Yes, please."

She starts to get out the moka pot and Dante gives me a look.

"She doesn't mess around," I say.

"Wow, I'm impressed," he says.

Ten minutes later, Rosalie is pouring Dante an espresso.

He takes a sip and his eyes roll back. "Oh. My. God. You are a master," he says.

Rosalie giggles. "I am good."

"What's the plan for today?" he asks.

"I thought we'd go to the beach for a long walk," I say.

"Perfect."

"Also, for whatever reason, Nico thinks you being here is enough of an occasion for a dinner party so he's invited the neighbors on each side to come over tonight." I roll my eyes, but I'm joking.

"Who are the neighbors?"

"I've only met the one guy, Wayne. He owns a high-end import business. The woman on the other side is a single mom. Her daughter is friends with Rosalie."

Rosalie gasps. "Is Julia coming, too?"

"I hope so," I say. "She's invited. That's for sure."

Rosalie frowns. "What if she's with her dad?"

"Then we'll have her over another time, okay?"

Nico comes out just then.

"When are you guys going to get out of my hair so I can start dinner preparations?"

Dante grins. "Are you sure you're not Italian? My Nonna would be up at 6 a.m. on Sundays starting the sauce for Sunday Supper. You sort of remind me of her right now."

Nico laughs and the booming sound fills my heart with joy.

"Soon," I say.

————

WE LEAVE Nico at the stove with Django at his feet waiting for scraps.

"What you making?" I ask before we walk out.

"You'll see," he says. He's being secretive about what he's making. I know whatever it is, Dante will be impressed. And Dante is a hard sell. As a chef and restaurant owner, his standards are crazy high, but after swooning over the chilaquiles last night, I know Nico will impress even Dante.

It's the perfect day to go to the beach. It's in the low 80s but there is this cool breeze that takes the edge off and makes it feel amazing. The three of us kick off our shoes and walk on the wet sand.

We walk about a mile and then I lead them up to a taco stand on the boardwalk. As we sit at the picnic table and eat fish tacos, I hold up a finger.

"Sssshh, don't tell your dad I took you here," I say to Rosalie. "He wants us to starve until supper, but I think Dante needed to have Rico's Tacos, don't you?"

She smiles. "For sure. They're the best."

Dante nods. "They're damn good."

We are sipping the rest of our drinks, *horchatas*, when Dante sighs loudly. "I can see why you like it here so much, Gia."

I nod. "I do miss the city, though," I say. "There's no place like San Francisco in the fall."

"That's a fact."

"Would you ever move down here?" I ask, turning to Dante. "You are one reason I'm keeping my loft. So I have a place in Northern California close to you."

He shrugs. "I used to think no way, but I've realized that I'm ready for a change."

I jump up and hug him. "Really? Really? You're not shitting me?"

"Um, I said maybe."

"You never said maybe."

"Well, I meant maybe."

Rosalie got bored with our conversation and is standing near the picnic table doing some martial arts moves.

"Wow, kid, you look like a pro," he says.

"I haven't even taken a class yet," she says proudly. "I've just been looking at videos online."

I look at Dante. "Her classes start next week. Nico doesn't know yet."

"Why's that?"

I shrug. "He wants Rosalie to have as normal a life as possible and doesn't think that should be part of it."

Rosalie is listening. I never hide things from her or say things she can't hear unless they are the worst of the worst.

Dante doesn't answer. My eyes widen. "Do you agree with him or something?" I say and frown.

"I don't know," he says. "I guess it depends on whether Rosalie wants to take martial arts classes."

"I do," Rosalie says. "I want to take them. My dad sometimes still treats me like a baby. I mean, I'm much more mature than most kids my age."

"That's true, honey."

She frowns now. "Do you think he'll say I can't take the classes?"

I think about it for a second and then say, "No. I think if you want to, he'll let you."

"Phew," she says.

"Let's head back."

———

WHEN WE GET HOME the large patio table in the back yard is already set and the house smells amazing.

I grab Rosalie and pull her onto my lap.

"So, tell me about your friend Julia."

"She's nice."

"Well, duh."

"Not like the girls at school."

I freeze but try not to let my reaction show on my face. Too late.

Rosalie tosses her hair. "I don't care anyway."

I turn her to face me. "What girls at school?"

"Just these girls in my class."

"Honey, what are they doing?"

She looks down.

"You can tell me. It's okay."

Dante and Nico are in the kitchen at the stove.

"I don't want my dad to worry."

"It's just me and you? Okay?"

"They make fun of me."

"What do they say?"

"We had to draw a picture and they call me weird now."

"What? Because of your picture?"

She nods. My heart is pounding now.

"What was the picture of?"

She shrugs.

"Is it here? At home?"

"I'll go get it." I wait at the table, tapping my fingers on the wood.

Rosalie comes back with a big white sheet of paper. It looks like it was crumpled up and then unfolded and straightened out. She hands it to me.

My heart breaks right then and there.

It shows a girl that is probably her hiding under a bed. And then a bunch of men with guns in the house. And then bodies. Bodies with heads off and blood coming out of them.

Again, I try not to react.

"What did the teacher say?" I ask. There's no grade on it.

"I didn't turn it in."

"Why not?"

"Because they were all making fun of me. They said I was a

freak. I didn't want Mrs. Cassidy to think that, too." A tear drips down her face.

I grab her and hug her.

I tamp down the anger starting to flare.

She doesn't need my angry indignation right now. She needs my love.

Nico happens to glance out the window right then and he raises an eyebrow. I just meet his eyes and barely shake my head.

"I'm sorry," I say. There is so much I want to say about how kids are cruel and those girls don't understand and that she's so special, but I just leave it at sorry.

She pulls away and crawls out of my lap. "But Julia doesn't think I'm a freak."

"Of course, she doesn't," I say, brightly. "Because you're not. And she's the one who knows you the best, right? Those other girls don't really know you."

Her head bobs up and down.

"What about Julia's mom?" I ask to change the subject. "Is she nice, too?"

Rosalie looks away. "Rosie?"

"She's nice I guess. Maybe too nice."

I laugh. "How can someone be too nice?" Inside, I'm thinking, holy shit this kid is smart.

"I can't explain. You'll see."

I smile. "Well, I for one can't wait to meet her and Julia."

4

THE CANDLES ARE LIT AND THE PARTY LIGHTS STRUNG throughout the yard are turned on, casting our patio in a magical light.

Dante and I are sitting out by the fountain with mojitos.

"I'd have thought you'd be a tequila girl by now," Dante says. "This is quite a frou-frou drink for you."

"Agreed," I say. "But there's something about this climate that makes me crave these. They make me feel like I'm on vacation."

"You are," he says. "Your life is one big vacation."

I can't argue. "Yours could be too," I say. "Your restaurants do just fine without you. You could live down here and be on vacation with me all year long."

He shakes his head. "I'd be bored."

"I highly doubt it."

Just then we hear voices in the house. I stand. "Time to meet the neighbors."

Dante smiles at me and adjusts the necklace he picked out. "Knock 'em dead. You look smashing."

He dressed me. Or I should say he bossed me into wearing

what he wanted me to wear. I always pretend to protest, but if I had my way he'd come over every morning and pick out my clothes for the day.

This afternoon he picked out a black maxi dress (my new uniform) but one of my fancier ones. This one is super deep cut and hugs the bodice and then is all flowy toward the ankles. He picked out this massive chunky turquoise and silver necklace to wear with it. He told me no eye makeup, just pinkish lipstick and my hair down. I always do as he says—when it comes to this stuff. So, I feel pretty confident that I look good when I go into the house to greet our guests.

But that confidence fades when I see what our neighbor looks like.

What the fuckity fuck?

I don't understand my reaction but I feel dowdy in my dress all of a sudden.

Django either senses my dismay or knows something I don't because he emits a low growl. I grab his collar. His fur is bristling. Dogs know shit. If you think they don't, you're fooling yourself. He doesn't like her.

The neighbor doesn't see me at first as she stands in our entry way. She's gushing all over Nico, which probably is partly why I suddenly feel like stabbing her. Her daughter, Julia, a tall girl with long brown hair is smiling and talking to Rosie off to the side.

I take in our neighbor even more. She wears a teeny tiny white miniskirt and has super tanned shapely legs that are unusually long even without the beige high-heeled sandals. Her tanned face is offset by brilliant white teeth and ice blonde hair that falls in a silky sheet to her shoulders. She has on a white low-cut tank top that hugs her huge boobs and creates quite an eyeful of cleavage. Her lips are pink pillows of injection at its finest. Her eyes are massive ice blue orbs with fake eyelashes.

I swear under my breath.

She looks like a fucking Playboy bunny. Or a high-class stripper.

This is the woman my husband hangs out with at the school bus stop two times a day five days a week? Fuck me.

If she dresses like this to a backyard barbecue, she probably wears a teddy to the fucking bus stop every day and practices her stripper moves on the street sign pole.

All of my insecurities as a girl in Monterey with dark hair and dark skin come flooding back to me. I was the "ethnic-looking" one among a sea of WASPy girls. I'm suddenly right back in junior high being called a Dago and a Wop.

Dante, who was there with me in junior high and is with me now, grips my arm tightly and says under his breath, "Stop that right now."

Rosalie and Julia are about to walk out. I grab Rosalie. "Do me a favor and take Django in your room with you, would you?" She nods and skips out.

I exhale and plaster a smile on my face as I step further into the room.

At first, she and Nico don't see me and this pisses me off. They are laughing about something.

Rosalie and Julia have disappeared into her bedroom with Django.

Then Nico looks up and sees me and his smile erases all of my insecurity and doubt.

"Gia!" he says. Then he turns to stripper mom. "Gloria, this is my ... this is ... Gia."

He stumbles on what I am. What am I? Not his wife. His lover. His partner? We've never really called it something by name.

I stick out my hand and she puts her wet noodle in it. I shake it firmly, meeting her eyes.

"The pleasure is mine," I say.

She looks away for a second and then withdraws her hand before smiling.

I see.

"This is Dante," I say.

"Charmed," he says taking her hand. She giggles and turns toward him. I can tell instantly she's thrilled to not have to look at me anymore.

I watch her face as she takes Dante in. I wonder if she can tell he's gay. It's not always obvious. She must not know because she is simpering and doing this thing where she juts her hip forward.

Then there is a knock at the door and Nico throws it open.

"I'm Damien," he says sticking out his hand. Dante gives me a look. I'd warned him that we use Nico's witness protection name. I know he invited Wayne himself, so he's probably just reminding him of his name and using it to remind me and Dante to stick to our stories.

"I'm Wayne," the man says. He's a good-looking guy with blonde hair swept back and a chiseled jaw. He looks a lot like Matt Damon and I think that even more when he smiles and nearly has the same dimples as the actor.

It takes me ten seconds to tell he's gay. Okay, yes, I'm basing it on his outfit. But no straight man is that stylish.

He has on a green sweater, fancy jeans and green suede loafers that probably cost as much as our monthly mortgage.

Dante clocks the designer clothes instantly and gives me a look.

Wayne and the woman exchange greetings, something like "nice to see you again," so I assume they've met.

"Would you like something to drink?" Nico asks Wayne.

"I don't drink alcohol but I'll take just about anything else you have."

"I have just the thing," Nico says and steps aside to introduce me.

"Wayne, I'd like you to meet Gia."

"Hi," he says and gives me a disarming smile.

"This is my best friend, Dante," I say. Dante steps forward and it's all over.

I see the way they take each other in.

They shake hands and then Dante does this swivel where he basically cuts Wayne off from the rest of us, so all we see is Dante's back. They are already deep in conversation.

Which means I have to deal with the stripper.

"What can I get you to drink, Gloria? We have red wine and a full bar."

She smiles and extracts a bottle of white. "I hope it's okay if we open the wine I brought."

Nico takes it from her. "I'll do the honors," he says and heads to the kitchen.

Leaving me and Gloria there to stare at each other.

"What do you do, Gia?" she asks.

"I own a nonprofit that helps the homeless," I say, taking a sip of my drink even as I know it's rude not to wait for her to get a drink. "And you?"

"I'm an attorney."

"Fascinating," I say. "What's your specialty?"

"Oh, boring stuff. Estate law. Things that would bore you to tears to talk about."

Nico appears with two glasses of white wine. He hands Gloria one and then takes a sip of the other. "Excellent," he says when he's tasted it. "A fine Pinot Gris."

"I do know my wines," she says smiling.

I hate how refined and sophisticated she is despite the stripper clothes. It makes me feel like a fucking hick. Nico always teases me that I don't know jack shit about wine. I like my booze hard. Drinking mojitos lately is like me eating tofu instead of steak.

I drain my glass.

Nico, always a gentleman, doesn't miss a beat.

"What can I get you, darling?" he asks. I keep my eyes on Gloria as I say with a smile, "Tequila. The Patron please."

"Coming up."

"Wayne?"

"I'll have another virgin," he says and then cracks up.

His laugh is infectious and we all laugh, too.

When Nico leaves, I clear my throat.

"Why don't we head to the patio?" I say, thinking that I hate this hostess shit.

A half-hour later, we are all settled on the patio with drinks in hand. Dante is drinking a fresh mojito that Nico made, Wayne is sipping on a virgin one, and I'm on my second tequila and feeling no pain. My favorite Afro-Cuban music is filtering through the speakers and as night falls, the party lights hanging over the patio make everything feel magical.

Wayne is telling us about his business. He stores and moves high-end furniture. Dante tells him about his restaurants.

Gloria tells us a story about when she was in her 20s and a model in Paris and accidentally walked in on the president's uptight wife getting spanked by her maid. Nico laughs uproariously.

Again, I feel like a hick.

I have nothing to add.

I mean, what am I going to talk about? Killing people?

I'm left out of the conversation nearly completely. Especially when they realize that Gloria and Nico were born the same year.

As soon as I hear this I think, "Man, she's had some major work done."

I stare and then see some telltale wrinkles around her neck.

You can lift the fuck out of your face, but the neck is usually a giveaway.

Nico and Gloria start talking about things from the 70s and 80s. I yawn, bored. They're so excited about some stupid band that they both saw in concert.

"Gia!" Nico says. "Gloria saw Queen live the same year I did."

"Really?" I smile tightly and pour myself another drink. Soon they are off onto something else. Some stupid TV commercials from the 80s.

Looking at the two conversations going on before me, I feel something I haven't felt in a while—lonely.

I hate feeling uncomfortable in my own house—in my own private sanctuary. Suddenly, I want Gloria gone. Having her over was the worst idea Nico ever had.

But he's so fucking entertained by her. As if she knows what I'm thinking she shoots me a glance, I raise an eyebrow and lift my glass to her.

I stand. "Anyone need a refresher."

Both Nico and Dante give me looks. I know what those looks mean. So, what if I'm a little unsteady on my feet, the only way I'm going to get through this night is more alcohol.

I'm feeling small and insecure—a very strange feeling for me. I don't like it.

Nothing else to do but get shit-faced.

An hour later I'm on Nico's lap. He shifts uncomfortably. Then laughs, but it's fake.

"Gia..."

"You don't need to make excuses for me," I say. "So what if I like my booze?"

I can feel him cringe at the crass word. Booze. But that's what it is.

Rosalie and Julia come in. Julia is yawning. "Mommy, I'm tired."

For a split second, I see something cross Gloria's face that is revealing. Annoyance. Her own kid being sleepy is annoying. Because it means she has to go home now and has to put someone else's needs ahead of her own. I file that away. And instantly decide my instincts—not liking her—were spot on and not just some odd surfacing of a jealous nature I didn't realize I had.

The moment passes and Gloria stands putting her arm around Julia. "Let's get you to bed then, sweetie."

We all stand.

Django, who followed the girls in, growls at Gloria, who jumps back.

But then Wayne jumps up and is all over my dog, hugging him and petting him and Django loses his mind, doing that uncontrollable wiggle that shows he's in love.

When those two get done slobbering all over each other with all of us watching, Wayne stands and says something to Dante.

"Time for me to go, too," Wayne says and then looks at me. "Would you mind if I stole Dante for a while? I've got some old vinyl I want to play for him."

I'm drunk so I can't help it and burst into laughter

Dante gives me a horrified look. But Wayne, God bless him, bursts into laughter, as well.

I sling my arm around his shoulders. "Wayne, I think we are going to make fabulous friends," I say. I only slur my words a little bit. And I'm pointedly ignoring Gloria who is standing there watching. Nico disappeared inside to make care packages of leftover food for our guests to take home with them. He's thoughtful like that. God, I love him.

We walk to the front door with my arm still around Wayne. He has his arm around my waist to support me because I might be a little off balance. I smile at him again. "I like you. You're fun."

He laughs again.

Like what's not to like about a guy who laughs all the time? I love this guy.

Dante has loosened up and taken the stick out of his ass and is smiling now, too.

I reach over to a small ceramic bowl on the entry way table and hand Dante a key ring. "Here, baby, let yourself in...whenever."

Then I turn to Gloria who is watching. "Nice to meetcha," I say. I know fully well that I'm saying it like I met her and am never going to see her again and I couldn't give a fuck. Because as far as I'm concerned, I don't need her in my house or back-yard ever again. Call me a bitch. I don't care.

It's my fucking home now, too, and I refuse to have someone in my sacred space who makes me uncomfortable in any way.

Wayne on the other hand? That dude's welcome over anytime.

Nico is back and has these cute little containers of food. He hands them to Wayne and Gloria who both kiss his ass. I don't care. I've got my arm around Dante. "Use protection," I whisper in his ear.

He rolls his eyes.

"I like him," I say.

He smiles. "Me, too."

"No, really," I say. "He's good people."

"I know, Gia."

He pulls away from me.

"Night."

He kisses me on the cheek. "You better drink a lot of water before bed and maybe take an aspirin or you are going to be hurting tomorrow, *mi cara*."

"I'm fine."

I turn and walk away as Nico sees Gloria out. Django gives her one last look and follows me to Rosalie's room. It's where his bed is. He's really her dog now. As soon as she came into our lives, Django became her familiar, if there is such a thing. He treats her like his master, but also his puppy.

Rosalie is already in bed reading a book. She yawns when I walk in. Django crawls up on the bed and settles himself at her feet.

I sit on the edge of her bed. "Did you have fun?" I ask.

She smiles. "Yeah. Julia is really nice."

"I'm so glad," I say.

Then she frowns.

"What is it?"

She shrugs.

I raise an eyebrow.

"She said her mom is a little weird."

"Obvi," I say.

"She says her mom has a room that's totally off limits."

I think about that. That is very interesting. I hear Nico coming. He pauses in the doorway. I want him to say his own goodnight, privately. I try really hard to not intrude on every moment he and Rosalie have together.

"Night, sweetie," I say and leave the room.

In our bedroom, I light some candles and put on a new little number I ordered online. It's blood red and fits like a dream. I pull on thigh-high stockings and my best fuck me heels. I figure that fucking Nico's brains out will get rid of any of the lingering feelings I have that made me feel left out.

I WAKE WONDERING how on earth I felt so lonely and insecure the night before.

Nico wakes me with coffee and toast.

"Gia, you are the love of my life," he says.

I smile. Nothing like hearing that first thing in the morning.

"How's your head?" he asks.

"Surprisingly fine," I say. "I did drink a lot."

"I noticed."

I don't answer. What's there to say?

"Dante here?"

"Yeah. He says he got home about two. No sex."

I laugh and practically spit out my coffee. "Thanks for the detailed report."

"He says they want to wait."

My eyes widen. "Holy shit. That's serious."

"That's what I said," Nico says.

After my breakfast in bed, I step out the French doors to the patio to finish my coffee. Dante is out there already on the chaise lounge. He's on the phone. I sit beside him. He's talking to his manager of his restaurants in Sausalito.

"What would I do without you?" he says to the man and winks at me. "Okay. Well, let me know if there's anything you need. Ciao."

He hangs up.

"Did your restaurants implode overnight without you there?" I say.

"Very funny." But he can't hide his grin.

"Spill it."

"He's really great." He shoots a quick glance over my shoulder to where our stone wall separates our yard from Wayne's.

"What's his house like?"

"Beautiful."

"Well the man clearly has good taste," I say.

"His style is impeccable," Dante says.

"Yeah, like his outfit was so coordinated."

"Totally," Dante says. "Which reminds me. I want to ask about his stylist. Or maybe he does it himself?"

Dante grabs his phone and dictates a text. "Good morning! Gia and I were sitting here on the patio having coffee and reminiscing about what a wonderful night it was and Gia said she wanted to know more about the outfit you were wearing so she can buy something similar for me for my birthday. She wants every detail. I apologize."

I practically spit out my coffee. "You liar!" I say and burst out laughing.

Dante grins and says, "Wait. He's typing."

"Okay."

Five minutes' pass and Dante is still looking at his phone.

"Um, how long does it take to say lime shirt and fancy jeans?" I ask.

"Oh, hush."

Finally, the text comes through. Dante reads it and smiles.

"What?" I say, suddenly suspicious.

"Here," he says and hands me the phone.

Wayne wrote a book. Like a fucking term paper. About. His. Outfit.

Tell her that it was a Dior sport top with an indented pattern stamped on the front from the Beverly Hills boutique. Awesome store. Nathaniel is my personal shopper and hand picks my style so well.

I wore it with Gucci tailored jeans, light sage Gucci loafers, matching Gucci belt, all from the San Francisco three-story department store. Cesar is my stylist and over the top in fashion perfect touch! Cesar is amazing because we have the exact same size in shirts, pants and shoes so he can try everything on for sizing and send me everything on consignment. I look at it, if I like it, I keep it. If I pass, I send it back. They send me the pre-shipping labels and then charge my card for whatever I am keeping.

Right around Thanksgiving he sent me a huge box. It was so heavy I could barely get it up the stairs. It had six outfits that were bagged individually in the zippered suit bags. Three pairs of shoes. Each one had socks, shoes, and a belt. When I called him I said I was so surprised at how much they sent me to try on. I said, 'Oh, my God, this is even too much for me to add up. What is it, like $25,000?' And then he said, 'No, Wayne, it's $25,015.' Lol.

It took me a week to go through each thing and then it was raining so I didn't send it back for like three weeks. The manager said for me not to worry about it. I think I ended up spending like 12k.

The jewelry accessories I had on were the new Gucci watch with the pattern down the band and across the top of the face gold – super pretty. And Tiffany box chain necklace with a green Russian demantoid pendant. Tiffany box bracelet, 1.5 carat round 3 diamond band. And the most important thing I was wearing was a Chakra Reiki Healing Heart Bracelet from a nonprofit raising money for food. Lol."

I'm speechless.

I hand Dante back the phone and say, "I'm not sure I've ever met anyone who is such a perfect match for you.

Dante blushes. Actually blushes.

"If it's okay with you, I'd like to invite him to dinner tonight. I'll cook."

"Hells yeah," I say. "If you are cooking, you can invite anyone you want."

I pause. "Except the other neighbor."

Dante raises an eyebrow. "Gia, I've never known you to be jealous."

"I'm not."

"You're not?"

"No," I say and stand.

"Why you running away?"

"Fuck you."

I say it jokingly, but Dante shakes his head.

"Gia. Nico is crazy about you. And if he's not, fuck him. Isn't that the Gia I know and love?"

I swallow.

He stands up and hugs me from behind, putting his chin on my shoulder.

"I know, sweetie. You love him. That means the stakes are high."

"I've loved other guys."

"Bobby."

"True."

"And Bobby never even said 'boo' to another woman when you were around."

"True."

"So, this is a new ball game. The man you love is very social, outgoing, and loves people."

"True," I say in a whiny voice.

"You're gonna have to deal."

"I don't want to," I say in a pouty voice.

"Gia, jealousy does not suit you."

"They just have so much in common."

"That's a problem?"

I disentangle myself from his embrace and turn to face him, thinking.

"No. That's not the problem. If I liked her, I would be thrilled about that and their friendship. I think it's something else."

Dante smiles. "Now, we're getting somewhere."

"She's not what she appears to be."

He just nods. "I know, baby. You and I can see it from a mile away. Nico can't. And that's okay."

I exhale loudly. "You sure?"

He nods. "You can trust him. And that's all you need to know."

I smile. "Thanks, Dante."

He brushes past me. "I'm heading to the store. Where's your local gourmet grocery store? I've got to get started."

"Dude, it's not even lunch time."

"Gia, let the maestro work."

After Dante leaves, Nico and I take advantage of Rosalie watching a Disney movie to go back to bed. I seriously cannot get enough of the man.

We are lying in bed after when he brings up something I've been avoiding.

"Gia? I know you are coming from the best place, the best intentions, but I want Rosalie to have a normal, American childhood."

I play dumb. "And? What are you saying?"

"The martial arts thing."

"The classes?"

"The classes."

"I had a normal, American childhood and I took martial arts classes."

He frowns.

"Nico, it's like signing a kid up for soccer, but better because it's also a mindset thing."

He is chewing his inner lip. A good sign. He's thinking. I trail my fingers across his bronze chest.

Finally, he exhales. Then he shrugs.

I hop out of bed. "She starts Tuesday."

He shakes his head.

I smile. "Trust me. It was one of the best things my dad ever did for me."

"If you say so," he says. But he is not smiling.

5

Dante knocks it out of the park with dinner.

It's a late dinner—which I personally love since it's totally European style—because Wayne works until seven every night.

When he shows up around eight he has a bouquet of flowers and a leather, I shit you not, picnic basket that he unpacks. He hands Dante a bottle of red wine, Nico, a box of Cuban cigars, and me, a bottle of Patron wrapped in a red ribbon. He obviously was paying attention last night. I kiss him on the cheek. Django loses his mind. I guess Wayne is his new best friend. Rosie thinks it's hysterical.

As far as I'm concerned, the dude is practically already family.

I would like him no matter what for his easy laugh but I really, really like him for the way he looks at Dante.

We are laughing so loud, I'm sure the whole block can hear us.

For a second, a tinge of guilt races through me. I'm sure Stripper Mom can hear us.

Whatever. If she wasn't so sketchy, I'd have gladly included her in our plans.

The rest of the week passes in a similar manner.

Wayne joins us around eight every night for a late dinner. After a stern talking to by me, Wayne dials it back on the hostess gifts, though, and only contributes wine every night–even though he doesn't drink it—and sometimes dessert.

Nico makes his specialty tamales one night.

I make the one recipe I can make: spaghetti and meatballs.

Dante takes over the other nights with his talents.

One day Wayne takes off work and he and Dante head to Mexico where they both get Botox and buy some fancy shoes. I can't believe how much alike they are. I love it.

The only night that is somewhat out of the ordinary is Tuesday when I take Rosalie to her first martial arts class.

I don't tell Nico but I paid extra for one-on-one training. This Dojo is normally closed on Tuesdays, but I made it worth it for the sensei to open for Rosalie.

The sensei is an older man. I read a book on my phone in the corner during the first lesson, but I'm attuned to what he is doing, as well. When the lesson is over, I'm satisfied I found the right sensei and bow deeply to him.

On the drive home I ask Rosalie what she thought.

"I love it," she says.

"Good," I say and smile.

I would not force her to go if she didn't like it. That would accomplish nothing.

Then it's Friday night. We order take-out pizza. As you do.

We sit out on the patio under the party lights and grape arbor and laugh.

I've never laughed so much. Wayne regales us with stories of his crazy youth before he became sober.

"Dude, you're a walking miracle," I say after hearing one harrowing story of him falling off a cliff and landing on a ledge. When he was a toddler, he accidentally got locked in an old refrigerator in a farm's barn. The only reason his mother found him in time was the family dog whined and led her to him.

"My mother says I have more lives than a cat," he says, grinning.

"Sounds like you do," I say.

Dante has his arm slung casually around Wayne's chair. He sits there and grins at everything Wayne says. Django lays at Wayne's feet. Traitor. Rosie doesn't seem to mind, though.

I share some stories of the trouble Dante and I got into growing up, but we stay away from any of the gloomy stuff. Because there is plenty of that.

And Nico skillfully talks about his childhood in Mexico without revealing anything about being a Cartel boss. It feels disingenuous, but it's how it has to be.

At one point, Rosalie comes out and asks if Julia can come over.

I look at Nico and say "I don't think so."

"Why?" she whines.

I wait to see if Nico is going to answer but he doesn't so I do. "It's late and it's a school night."

Rosalie gives me the nastiest look I've seen from her. She crosses her arms. "That's not fair."

I shrug. "Maybe not."

She continues to glare at me. I look at her calmly.

Finally, she gives a big huff and turns and stomps off. Django unfolds himself from Wayne's feet and follows her.

Nico is trying not to laugh.

Finally, when she is inside, he shakes his head.

"*Aye Yai Yai.*"

"She's your kid all right," I say.

He laughs.

Dante turns to Wayne. "What do you know about the neighbor?" he asks in a low voice jutting his chin at the tall wall separating our yard from hers.

"I know Django hates her," I add. They all ignore me.

Wayne leans in. "I don't know much. I've only lived here a little over a year. She usually keeps to herself. That's why I was surprised to see her here the other night. When we had our annual block party last year, everyone else told me she never comes. But I do know she's had some tragedy in her life."

Nico frowns. "Like what?" he asks.

I watch him carefully. But I refuse to be jealous. Refuse.

"Her son died of an overdose a few years ago. Heroin."

Nico's face blanches. I quickly glance at Wayne but I don't think he's noticed.

"I think that's what destroyed her marriage to Julia's dad," he says. "Julia was only a baby at the time."

"I wonder if maybe the marriage was already on the rocks?"

I mean, who has kids fifteen years apart unless maybe they were trying that whole time, which is incredibly sad. Or if they thought having a baby would revive their marriage. It seemed absurd but I knew people did it.

"Poor Julia," I say in a neutral voice, still watching Nico.

I know that he takes personally every overdose death. As the former head of one of the world's most powerful cartels, he was likely behind the availability of most drugs in the U.S. I've told him that yes, that sucks, but that he also isn't the one holding a gun to people's heads making them do drugs. At the same time, a kid overdosing is the worst. Are their brains even formed enough to make a rational decision if the drug is available? Doubtful.

I'm about to change the subject for Nico's sake, when Wayne says something else.

This time he leans forward and whispers. "There was some

talk after her second husband disappeared that maybe she had something to do with it."

"What?" Now, I'm leaning forward.

"He was quite well off. She had him declared dead after five years and inherited all his millions."

"How did he disappear?" I ask. "I mean what were the circumstances?"

Wayne shrugs. "I never really heard most of it. When I moved in last year, she'd already inherited everything. I think it had just been five years or something."

"Very interesting."

Nico stands and asks if he can refill our drinks.

I know he's done with this conversation. Hearing about the overdose ruined it for him.

Wayne stands. "Thanks, but I think it's time for me to let you guys get some sleep," he says and then turns to me. "If you guys don't have plans, I'd love to take you out on the bay tomorrow on my boat."

Nico grins. "Fantastic. I'm in." He looks at me.

"I'm in!" I say, relieved to see his smile.

Dante stands, as well. "I'm staying over at Wayne's, but I'll be home bright and early to wake you guys up."

The sleepovers have happened a few times this week. I think they are getting serious.

I love Wayne, but it also feels really fast.

Then again, who am I to judge? I fell for both Bobby and Nico, the two loves of my life, in days.

After they leave, Nico and I stay out on the patio. I hear some music and voices coming from the Stripper's backyard. It's late. I can only hope she didn't hear our whispering earlier. But with our small water fountain and our own music, I know there is no way.

"Sounds like Gloria has company," I say in a low voice.

Nico doesn't comment.

"Nico, you can't feel responsible for every overdose death, baby."

He swallows and nods. "I know, but I still do."

"You can't do that to yourself," I say reaching for his hand.

"I feel sorry for her," he says.

"What?" I say, knowing full well I'm opening a fucking can of worms.

He shrugs. I wait until he explains, trying not to get pissed off.

"When I see her at the bus stop every day, she asks if we are having parties every night. She must hear us."

"Oh well," I say.

He shakes his head. "I feel bad that we don't invite her."

"I don't. She didn't invite us to her house tonight did she? Or any other night for that matter."

"Gia..."

"We don't owe her a damn thing. Especially not an invitation into our house. Nothing. Even if her son died of an overdose, Nico."

He frowns.

"Nico," I say, making sure he is looking at me. "I don't like her. I don't want her in my house."

We've been keeping our voices low, but I raised mine a little too much. I glance over at the wall as if I can see through it. I still hear her laughing and music so I relax.

"She wanted to bring by a dessert on Sunday," he says. I freeze.

My eyes widen. "I'm not stupid," I say in a low whisper. "She's trying to finagle a dinner invite for Sunday? No fucking way. Did you tell her it was okay?"

He simply nods. But his jaw tightens. He is not happy.

"Sorry, you're going to have to tell her that our plans have changed."

His face grows dark. Nobody tells Nico what to do. Even I'm careful about that. He was the head of a cartel, for crying out loud. He's used to being the boss, the one telling others what to do.

I get out of my chair and sit on his lap, straddling him. I take his face in my hands.

"I'm not trying to tell you what to do," I say. "It's just that my home is my sanctuary. For me, I have to absolutely feel 100% comfortable with the people who I invite into my home. I hope you understand. I wanted to like her. I really did. But I'm not comfortable with her in our home."

He looks at me for a few seconds before he answers.

"I will respect your wishes."

"Thank you," I say and feel relief wash over me. I don't want to fight with Nico over it. But I also can't give in on this.

"I will tell her tomorrow," he says.

And with those words, I know I've made an enemy.

One who lives right on the other side of my backyard wall.

6

Wayne's "boat" borders on a small yacht. It has a master bedroom, living room, galley kitchen, and bathroom below deck.

After we leave shelter of the marina, Wayne takes us over to the USS Midway Museum. It's an actual aircraft carrier loaded with planes. We slowly cruise past taking in the planes. There are fighter jets and helicopters and other restored planes.

Then he goes full throttle as he takes us out on the bay. It feels amazing to have the wind blowing in my hair. Rosalie seems to love it, too. She keeps smiling at me as we speed out to a spot to anchor for our picnic.

Finally, we are away from other boats and Wayne drops anchor. We crawl up onto the deck and have a picnic that Dante prepared of grapes and brie and caviar and crackers.

All of us are in bathing suits and after we eat, we spread out and soak up the sun.

I drift off, lulled to sleep by the gentle rocking of the sea.

Rosalie is between me and Nico and is reading a book. Sunbathing is boring when you are eleven, I'm sure.

I'm woken by Nico kissing my shoulder.

I smile up at him. "This is the life," I say.

He grins down at me. "I could not be happier."

I glance over at Wayne and Dante. They sit side-by-side staring out at the sea.

"I think they feel the same."

Nico smiles.

Wayne has already invited Dante to stay the night on the boat. He'd explained that every Friday and Saturday he has a "sleep-over" at the marina. It's like a mini vacation.

Dante is all in.

We only head back to the marina when the sun is dipping low on the horizon and a chilly breeze kicks up. I wrap Rosalie in a soft blanket as we head back and pull the hood of my hoodie up.

The sun has set by the time we pull back into the marina and there is a party at the boat docked next to Wayne and the one beside that.

We hop out and Wayne introduces us.

The boat next to his is much smaller and needs a paint job.

A girl with jean shorts on, a bikini top and frizzy blonde hair runs up and hugs Wayne.

"When are you going to come to dinner?" she asks. "We are grilling tonight."

"Soon," he says. "These are my friends."

He introduces us. Her name is Shelby. Two guys come up from the other boat. One guy looks like a has-been quarterback with a beer belly. He has a thick head of hair and a red face, probably from a few too many beers today. He is holding a bottle of beer as he nods his hellos. His face is tight and closed and I don't like the way he looks at me when we are introduced. His name is Bryce Gordon. I can tell by Nico's tight "Hello" and body language, he doesn't like Bryce much either.

The other guy seems harmless. A tall, thin guy with long hair, a beard, and a moustache introduced as Michael Ballard.

They're both shitfaced.

And then I realize that Shelby is, too.

She just hides it better.

Wayne has already explained that even though he's staying the night out here tonight, he already has dinner plans. I guess he's ordered room service for him and Dante from the hotel attached to the marina. Which is fucking insane. You can have room service on your boat in the marina.

But Shelby is making it tough for him to refuse.

"Come on, Wayne," she says and whines, hanging on his arm. "Give me a day you'll have dinner with us. Come on! Why can't you tonight? You said you're staying the night, right?"

Bryce reaches out and grabs her arm, which I find strange.

"Come on, Shelby," he says. "Wayne will come when he has time. He said he already has dinner plans tonight. Right?"

He shoots a glance at Wayne. And then his eyes rove over me, Dante, and then linger on Nico. It sends a chill down my spine. He takes Nico in from head to foot. Nico is leaning down talking to Rosalie.

"I'll be here later this week to meet a guy doing some work on the boat," Wayne says. "Maybe Thursday?"

"See you then," she says.

Bryce is now looking at Wayne. He smiles then and it unnerves me. Something is wrong with that guy.

When we are walking back to the parking lot, I ask Nico if he caught any weird vibes off the dude.

"I'm sorry, Gia, I wasn't paying attention. Rosalie was talking to me."

That's unlike Nico. He usually clocks everything around him. That worries me. He's become complacent in this new life.

Rosalie skips ahead to the car. I wince, but I say it, "Do you think he recognized you?"

Nico stops. He turns to face me and puts his hands on my shoulders.

"Gia, I love you for always being vigilant and looking out for me," he says. "But I worry about you. I worry that you can never relax."

I feel a sob rise in my throat. He's right. I don't ever feel like I can relax.

"You didn't answer my question," I say.

Nico smiles. "No, I don't think he recognized me. I watched him very carefully when we were introduced. He does not know who I am."

I can feel my body relax in relief. Of course, Nico checked him out immediately and gauged his response. Only then did he relax.

"I'm sorry for doubting how careful you are," I say.

He wraps his arm around me. "You never, ever, need to apologize for caring about me and loving me, Gia."

God, I love this man. But I still have a lingering doubt about that Bryce guy.

I don't know what's up with him, but I know he's up to no good.

7

The next few weeks pass in a leisurely fashion.

Wayne has a new client and project and is very busy at work, so we only see him for dinner once or twice a week. However, Dante sleeps over at his place more often than not.

And then on the weekends, the two of them disappear down to the marina from Friday night to Sunday morning.

Every Thursday night, Dante and Wayne take Rosalie out for dinner to some fancy restaurant.

"We want to expose the girl to the fine things in life," Dante says.

"Why does that feel like an insult?" I say.

He laughs. "It's not."

"Whatever."

But Rosalie always comes back amped up.

"I tried snails, Gia!"

"Escargot," Dante corrects.

"Yes, escargot. And caviar. And truffles."

"Very fancy," I say and smile. "You're lucky to have Dante as an uncle."

"And Wayne," she says in a matter-of-fact voice.

"Yep," I say and shoot a glance at Dante over her head. He turns red.

When Nico is putting her to bed that night, I drag Dante out on the patio with a bottle of wine.

"Spill it."

"I know it's crazy, but I think he's the one."

I smile. "I think so, too."

We sit there giving each other shit-eating grins until Nico comes out.

———

THE NEXT DAY, the school calls Nico. It's getting close to the time that Nico leaves to get Rosalie at the bus stop. At first I think that the call is just saying the bus is late—that happens sometimes. But I can tell immediately from Nico's expression it's not that. He hangs up and grabs his keys.

"Nico?" I ask, alarmed. "What's going on?"

"They say she's fine, but I need to pick Rosalie up from the nurse's office."

"Oh, my God. I'm coming, too."

But I'm in my underwear with my hair wet. We'd just made love and I'd taken a shower right afterward. I'd just got out of the shower and was about to blow dry my hair when the phone rang.

He hesitates, a coiled ball of tension. I look down at myself and then say, "Go. Call me please when you know what's going on."

He nods and races out.

I get dressed and wait, holding my phone for some word from Nico.

My stomach is in a knot. I keep reminding myself that they had said Rosalie was fine. So, what the fuck was going on?

Finally, I hear Nico's car pull in the driveway.

I meet them at the front door, coming out onto the front porch.

I hug Rosalie, but she hurries inside. Django is waiting. He whines when he sees her but then she slams the front door on him. We are still standing outside.

I turn to Nico. "Why didn't you call?" I say.

"I didn't want to talk in front of Rosalie."

"What's going on?"

"Rosalie was jumped."

"Jumped? What does that even mean? She's in fucking elementary school."

"A group of girls cornered her in the bathroom and hit her."

"Motherfucker," I say. "Is she okay?" I turn toward the house. He reaches for my arm.

"She's fine. She says she was able to fend them off. For the most part." He sighs. "I guess it is good to do the martial arts. She did some defensive move she'd learned."

I can't help but feel a little smug.

"Martial arts are great for defending herself against other little girls, but if she's going to really be able to take care of herself she needs to learn how to handle swords and guns. I should call Eva."

Nico whirls with an alarmed look.

"Absolutely not!" he says. "She should be playing with dolls not learning how to fight."

I can tell the words slipped out. I can't imagine Nico ever saying something like that if he'd thought about it first. I am fucking furious. How did I not realize the man I loved was a sexist pig?

"You're fucking kidding, right?" I say. "I mean what kind of sexist bullshit is this? You brought a child into your violent world and now you're complaining because she needs to learn to defend herself. Even if that didn't happen at school, she needs to learn self-defense simply because she's your daughter. Don't you get that? My aunt can teach her everything she needs to know."

My aunt Eva Santella. She's the Queen of Spades. A mob boss. A trained killer. A vigilante assassin. A woman that people around the world turn to when they need help.

Her villa in Italy is a boot camp/training ground for women assassins.

Nico knows all this.

His face is red. His hands are balled in fists at his sides.

"I am a new man. Nobody knows who I am."

I raise an eyebrow. "We don't know that for sure. And we don't know that it will remain that way forever, do we? Rosalie needs to be prepared."

"Excuse me?" a voice says.

I fucking jump.

It's the woman from next door. I can feel my face go icy. How much has she heard?

"I didn't see you or Rosie at the bus stop and I was worried," she says.

I bristle at her calling Rosalie by our nickname.

I can't deal with her. Not right now. If Nico wants to be friends with her, he can explain. I have nothing to say.

I turn and walk in the house without a word.

8

ON THURSDAY NIGHT, WE GRILL HOT DOGS AND HAMBURGERS OUT on the patio.

Dante is there. Wayne is staying over on the boat tonight. He has an early morning meeting with a man who is going to paint the boat.

"You going to survive a night without Wayne?" I ask, refilling his wine glass.

He grins. "He did invite me to stay on the boat tonight."

"Why didn't you?"

Dante shrugs. "I don't know."

"You bored already?" I ask.

"Hardly," he says and takes a swig of wine. "I just think maybe we might be moving too fast."

I lean forward and look him in the eyes. "Dante..."

He looks away.

"You're scared," I say.

He doesn't meet my eyes but he nods.

I get up and sit in his lap and put my arms around him. He buries his face in my shoulder. I whisper in his ear, "Baby, I promise, it's okay to love again. I promise."

"I can't lose someone else," he says in a choked voice.

"I know, baby. I know." I hug him tightly.

"I told him we should take a break," he says.

I pull back. "Is that what you want?" I ask.

He shakes his head.

"Well, you need to tell him. Call him now."

"It's too late. He said he was going to bed early tonight."

"Well, then first thing tomorrow. Get up, go down there with lattes and croissants and surprise him for breakfast and tell him how you feel."

I get up and look down at him. He is smiling.

"I know it's hard," I say. "God knows, I know it. But look at how it turns out when you make yourself vulnerable and let yourself love again."

We both look over at Nico and Rosalie.

Rosalie is busy practicing her martial arts moves near the grill. Well, far enough away that she won't get too close to the hot surface, but close enough for her dad to admire her moves. Django watches her through half-closed eyes.

"Daddy, watch this," she says and executes a move that makes me proud.

The kid is a natural.

"Wow," Nico says. "That was pure grace."

"Thanks," she says and smiles.

Nico meets my eyes and says, "I think having you take these classes was a great idea by Gia. She is a very smart woman."

I shake my head and mouth "kiss ass."

He laughs.

I get up and wrap my arms around him from behind. I whisper in his ear, "You know what really turns me on?"

"Do tell," he says.

"A man who can admit when he's wrong."

———

THE NEXT MORNING, I sleep in late. When I wake, Rosalie is long gone to school and Nico left a note that he was going to go hit some balls at the putting range. Dante is in the kitchen drinking coffee. Django is in the corner, keeping a close eye on him as he paces. He seems agitated.

Dante pours me a cup.

I smile at him, but he frowns.

"What's up?"

"Wayne hasn't returned my calls. When we aren't together, he usually calls to tell me good night, but he didn't last night. And when I tried him this morning his phone went right to voice mail. I've been trying not to freak out. I called his office and they haven't seen him, either."

"That's strange," I say.

I look away to hide my frown. I lean over and pluck a banana out of the fruit bowl on the counter. "Maybe he drank too much and passed out."

"He doesn't drink, remember."

"Oh, yeah," I say. "Duh."

"Can I borrow the Lincoln? I'm going down to the marina to make sure everything is okay."

"Want some company?" I ask.

He smiles. "Sure."

———

DANTE LETS us into the gate surrounding the marina with a key card.

"Wow," I say. "That's like someone giving you the keys to their house."

"Got those, too."

"Of course, you do."

Wayne's boat is in its slip. As we head down the steps to the docks, I see the boat on the other side of Wayne's pull out of its slip. It's pretty far away, but I can see that the woman, Shelby, is behind the wheel. I can't see anyone else on the boat.

We make our way down the dock to Wayne's slip.

I wait while Dante goes to the rear of the boat and steps on.

"Wayne?" he says. "You here?"

Then he disappears from my view.

I watch the woman navigate her boat toward the opening to the bay. When she gets to the end of the row, she turns and looks at me. Weird.

Dante pops back out.

"His bed wasn't slept in." As he speaks he looks around.

"Does he have any friends down here he might have stayed with?"

Dante shakes his head. "I don't think so. I mean, he mentioned he was going to have dinner with the neighbor."

He looks over at the empty slip.

"She just took off when we got here. I didn't see anyone else on the boat, but there could've been someone underneath."

Dante frowns.

"She gave me a weird vibe," I say. "I hate to even ask, but does Wayne swing both ways?"

"I don't think so," Dante says. "But even if he did, well, we had this conversation the other day, and we decided to become exclusive."

"Holy shit," I say. "But you live in Northern California?"

"I've been meaning to talk to you about that," he says. "I think I'm going to move in with Wayne."

"Wow. That's amazing. But what about— "

"My restaurants? You were right. They are humming along

fine without me. I've put the right people in place and they are kicking butt."

I had been holding my breath asking him about the restaurants or how long he was going to stay in San Diego because frankly, I was terrified he'd leave if I brought it up. Stupid I know.

I grabbed him in a big hug. "Oh, my God! This is the best news ever!"

He smiles at me. "We're going to open a place down here together."

I can't stop grinning but then his smile fades.

"Gia, I'm worried. Wayne isn't the flaky type."

"Is there any chance he came home last night and is at his house?"

"Maybe," Dante frowns. "But the door to the cabin wasn't locked. That's not like him. I locked it. And why isn't he answering his phone?"

I give one last glance to the opening to the bay where Shelby disappeared. I have a feeling she knows where Wayne is, but I keep my mouth shut. For now.

"Let's head home and you can check his house."

But Dante comes back from Wayne's house increasingly agitated. His brow is furrowed and he looks pained.

"Gia, I'm really worried."

"Do you know any of his friends that you can call?"

He shakes his head.

Nico comes in to the kitchen where we sit at the bar counter. He just got back from picking Rosalie up at the bus stop. She grabbed a snack and went straight to her room, saying, "I have soooo much homework."

Dante and I didn't say anything about Wayne. I don't want her to worry, too.

"What about his parents?" Nico asks. "Maybe you can call them and ask if they know any friends in the area."

"Yeah. I think he has his mom's number on his refrigerator," Dante says. "He'd left it there for someone who was house sitting once."

Ten minutes later, Dante comes back with his phone to his ear.

"Mrs. Clark? This is a friend of Wayne's. My name is Dante. Hey, I was just trying to reach him about something important and can't get through so I was wondering if you might have a phone number for some of his friends here in San Diego."

He left his number and hung up.

"Something important?" I ask.

"I don't want to leave a message that gives her a heart attack, Gia."

"Good idea."

We eat dinner on the patio, but Dante just picks at his food and checks his phone approximately one billion times.

Rosalie seems to sense what's going on. She looks from one face to the other. And then she frowns. Django emits a soft whine.

"You guys think I'm a baby. And that I don't know something's wrong. That's not fair."

I look at Nico. This is his call.

He reaches for her hand. "You're right. It's not fair. We are all worried about Wayne because he is not returning Dante's calls and we are not sure where he is."

Rosalie's reaction makes me jump.

Her chair screeches back and she throws her fork and knife across the table and races into the house screaming, "I hate this family. I hate San Diego. I hate all of you."

Django gives us a doleful look and then heaves himself up to follow her. He's such a loyal dog.

Nico starts to push back his chair, but then looks at me.

"Do you want to try talking to her?"

I nod. "I know she's only eleven, but these days girls are getting hormonally insane much younger than they used to. Teenage temper tantrums aren't unusual."

"And you know this how?" Nico says with an amused smile.

"My best friend Google."

He nods.

Inside, I find Rosalie sprawled across her bed her face buried in the pillows. Django is curled on the foot of her bed.

I sit down on the edge without saying anything and rub her back.

She swats my hand away.

I try not to laugh.

What a spitfire! I love it. I love her.

But then the smile disappears. She's worried about Wayne.

This kid has lost more people she's cared about before puberty than anyone I know. It breaks my fucking heart.

"He's fine, I'm sure," I say in a low voice.

She sits up and glares at me. "How do you know? How do you know, Gia?"

The disdain in her voice as she says my name stings, but I try not to take it personally. The kid is hurting. And scared.

"I know you're afraid. I am, too. I'm not going to lie to you. You deserve more than that."

"So where is he then? And how can you tell me he's fine!? Just leave my room. Just LEAVE!" She screams the last word.

I stand, reluctantly and she points her finger at the door. "Leave me alone!"

She is shaking and her face is red.

I nod. I am tempted to give her a fucking major lecture on respect and how she is talking to me, but I let it go. I pause at the door. "Rosalie, I'm here when or if you need to talk."

She simply folds her arms across her chest and glares.

I come back out to the patio.

"It sounded like it went well," Nico says and shakes his head.

I exhale loudly. "Yeah, she's pissed. And scared."

Dante stands. "I've got to do something, I'm going crazy here."

He looks around wild-eyed.

"Want to go for a drive? Or down to the beach?" I stand.

He nods. "Yes, but can I go alone? I'm not good company right now."

"Of course," I say.

He heads inside.

"Fuck," I say.

Nico raises an eyebrow.

"I swear if something happened to Wayne, I don't think he could take it," I say. "And I'm freaked out about Rosie. She can't lose someone else, either."

9

IT GROWS LATE AND WE HAVEN'T HEARD BACK FROM DANTE.

I'm wondering if I should worry about him now, too.

But I'm going to let him do his thing.

Nico and I go to bed. We are sound asleep when Dante wakes us, throwing open our bedroom door and rushing into our dark room.

He's distraught and on the verge of hysteria.

"Wayne's parents say his phone shows he's at the hospital."

"Maybe he's visiting someone there who is sick or injured," I say and sit up, turning on the bed side light. Nico sits up, too.

Dante has his phone to his ear. He starts talking.

"May I speak to the nurse on duty please?"

I stare at him. How did he know to even ask that?

"Yes, my name is Dante Montego. I'm a reporter with the San Diego Examiner. I'm calling to check the condition of a patient, Wayne Clark."

Then he collapses onto the floor.

———

WAYNE IS in critical condition in the ICU.

I finally get it out of Dante and hang up the phone for him.

I pull on leggings and a tee-shirt and Dante and I are out the door in two minutes flat. I have to drag Dante up from the floor of our bedroom. Nico follows me in a robe. "Stay with Rosie," I say even though it's a given.

I kiss him. "I'll call as soon as I know anything," I say. I turn. Dante is gone.

I find him in the passenger seat of the Lincoln in our garage.

Thank God for GPS that gets us to the hospital in ten minutes. I let Dante out front while I park. Inside, I check in and head to the ICU floor.

Dante is there. He's pacing.

He jumps when I put my hand on his arm.

"What did they say?"

"They don't know anything yet."

"Oh, my God."

"Wayne's family is in Missouri," Dante says.

I explain this at the front desk and we are told to wait.

Dante calls them. They are catching the next flight out.

The nurse says they can only give information about Wayne to family members. And that only family members can see him.

We wait and wait.

Two hours later, when Dante is practically hysterical with worry, a doctor takes pity on us. He stops in the family waiting area and asks for the family of Wayne Clark.

I'm pretty sure he knows we aren't family, but he takes us both into a small room and closes the door. Once the door closes, he begins to talk.

It's awful.

Wayne is alive.

But has suffered a severe brain injury.

He probably will not survive the night.

Dante's entire body slumps and he starts to hyperventilate.

"His brain is swelling without stopping. We did a scan and it has moved over 6 millimeters from where it is normally. Even if he does survive, there is a large probability he will suffer brain damage. There are areas of his brain that are gray in the scan. That is usually brain tissue that is dead."

I feel as if I'm going to vomit.

"What happened? How did this happen?"

The doctor flips through some papers.

"The 911 caller reported that he was found unconscious at the bottom of a flight of stairs at the marina. That's all we know. He has injuries to the front of his head and the back, which make it unlikely that he suffered a fall, but not impossible. He also has a black eye, which also leads me to believe the injury was not simply from falling down the stairs."

"Oh, my God." The implication of what he just said floors me. "He was attacked."

The doctor's face remains expressionless but he says, "That is a possibility."

"What about the police?" I ask. "Are they investigating?"

"I don't know."

Dante sits there like a zombie.

"What is going to happen next? With Wayne?" he asks. "I don't understand."

"We're monitoring the swelling around his brain," the doctor says. "If he survives the night and the swelling hasn't stopped, we will operate tomorrow. We will remove a portion of the skull to relieve the swelling. We'll know more in the morning."

"Can I see him?" Dante asks.

The doctor nods, but then glances at me. "One at a time, I think."

The "I think" means I can go in if I want so I turn to Dante.

"Are you okay with that?" I ask, squeezing Dante's hand. "Me waiting here or would you prefer I come with you?"

"I'll be okay," he says. His face is ashen. He leaves with the doctor.

I call Nico and tell him what I know, which is next to nothing.

"He's in a coma with a severe head injury. The brain is swelling and if it gets worse, they are going to operate and take out a portion of his skull."

"Good God."

I don't answer.

"I will tell Rosalie the bare minimum. When will you be home?"

"Not sure," I say. "I'll call you after we talk to the doctor again in the morning."

Twenty minutes later Dante comes back. He's been crying.

"It's bad. He looks so bad."

I hug him.

He's sitting with his head in his hands.

"What time do his parents get here?" I ask.

"I don't know. Like eight in the morning or something. They're taking a red eye."

"Good."

If any decisions need to be made about anything, his parents need to be here. I don't say this to Dante. Because the only big decision I think would have to be made is whether to pull him off life support if he's brain dead.

Thinking this makes me ill. Poor Wayne. Poor Dante. I'm worried sick. But I'm trying not to show this. I'm trying to be strong for Dante.

I drift off to sleep in the family waiting area and when I jerk awake, Dante is still sitting there, eyes wide, foot tapping. He is running on pure fear and adrenaline. I know he won't rest until he gets good news.

I just hope there will be some good news.

The doctor comes to find us early in the morning. I leap up horrified by the look on his face.

He takes a deep breath and asks when Wayne's parents are arriving.

"About nine is the earliest they could get here," Dante says.

I'm holding my breath, clutching Dante's arm. I want to be holding onto him in case he collapses.

The doctor purses his lips together and says, "He made it through the night. But it's not looking good. We've scheduled surgery for this afternoon."

"Thank God, thank God, thank God," Dante says. He gives me a sad smile. "He's going to be okay. They'll do the surgery and then he'll be okay."

I sit there in silence. Removing part of the skull is a last resort move to save his life. But I'm not going to tell Dante that. Not right now, at least.

Not long after, Wayne's parents rush past the family waiting room. I can tell it's them. They look like Wayne. Or rather, Wayne looks like them. They are both shorter, with the same blonde hair and athletic build that Wayne has.

Dante goes to the door and looks out after them. Then he settles back down.

Forty-five minutes later or so, they come into the family waiting room. Their faces are filled with grief. Dante stands.

The mother comes over to him. "Are you Dante?"

He nods. She just collapses in his arms.

Then the father comes over and slaps Dante on the back. "Thank you for calling us immediately."

"Of course," Dante says.

I stand. "I'm Gia, Wayne's neighbor, can I get you a coffee? I'm heading to the cafeteria?"

"Yes, please," the dad says.

I come back with a drink carrier full of coffees and cream and sugar.

Everyone grabs one.

Wayne's mother smiles at me. "I'm sorry, my name is Cheryl and this is my husband, John."

I smile and nod.

"I was just telling Dante here that it is a pleasure to meet him. Wayne has talked of nothing else since they met." She has a slight twangy accent that makes me instantly like her. I don't know why. She smiles and I want to hug her. It's that same contagious smile that Wayne has. You can't help but smile back.

Wayne has talked of nothing else since they met. I look over at Dante. I can tell he's fighting tears.

"That's great," I say, "Because it's definitely mutual. And I can say that from the minute Wayne walked in our house, we all fell in love with him. Dante. Me. My husband, Nico, and our daughter, Rosalie."

Dante shoots me a look. It is the first time I've ever said that — "our daughter, Rosalie."

But damn it, it feels natural. I'm going to own it.

"I'm so sorry that Wayne didn't have you in his life longer," the mother says and starts to cry.

Dante springs up out of his seat. "What? What do you mean?"

The father stands and puts his hand on Dante's arm. His face is crinkled with confusion. "Didn't the doctor tell you?"

I am up now, standing by Dante, ready to react. Filled with horror.

"Tell me what?" Dante says.

"They don't think our son is going to make it."

"The doctor came in while we were there," the mother says.

"He said that last night, but I thought ..." I trail off.

Dante whirls and runs down the hall. We watch, open-mouthed.

It's only then that I realize with horror, this is a repeat of what Dante has already been through. Except last time it was Matt. It was in Positano, Italy. And Matt died.

MUFFLED *popping sounds came from inside the hotel at the same time the woman on the balcony beside me screamed. It took me a split second to realize the popcorn sounds were gunshots. With horror, I realized that everyone I loved was inside: where the gunshots came from.*

Before I could react, the four men, now clearly wielding guns, raced outside. One of them shot a glance up at me before he joined the others, hopping on their bikes and squealing away. Stunned, I watched, unable to move, my feet felt nailed to the balcony. Distantly, somewhere in my head, I knew I needed to get inside. When the gunman had looked at me, I knew that I should duck or run, but I'd been frozen. The signal to move short-circuited on the way to my limbs...

Heart pounding with terror, I was finally able to move. I spun and ran into the hotel. From the top of the staircase on the second floor, I could see people on the first floor running and screaming, covered in blood. Others were carrying bleeding people. Somewhere in the chaos below me were the people I loved most.

Bobby. Dante. Matt. Mrs. Marino.

Down on the first floor, people stumbled around in a daze, some with blood spattered on their faces. Others clutching their sides or limping. I pushed through them. Voices and screaming came to me down a long tunnel. Sounds echoed and distorted. I pushed through the lobby toward the French doors leading to the courtyard.

Stepping into the courtyard, my mind couldn't process what I saw. Bodies on the ground. Some people crouched over them. Mrs. Marino shrieking, holding her head and wailing in an unintelligible lamentation. My eyes pivoted down. She stood over someone on the ground. Someone with fair hair covered in blood. Matt. In an instant, I registered that the man kneeling by Matt's prone body was Dante. Stunned, I scanned the bodies, panic rising like a tidal wave in my throat. Over by the bar ... facedown. A familiar silky auburn head. Gray silk shirt now dark with blood.

Time distorted. Voices undulated. Then all noise stopped. I could no longer hear. My vision blurred. I blinked, not taking my eyes off the pale cheek now resting on the cobblestones.

I stared, willing him to move. Straining my eyes to see his body move with a breath taken and a breath exhaled.

Movemovemove. Please move, Bobby. Please move. Please move. Please move. Please move.

After staring at him for a million years, I willed myself toward him. He could still be alive. He could still be alive. He could still be alive. But as I drew closer, his features came into focus. His mouth open with a slight trail of blood coming from it. His eyes staring at nothing.

My legs gave way and I collapsed onto the ground a few feet away from him. My hearing returned with a far-away keening sound piercing the strange silence in my head. Splayed on the ground, I lifted my head and looked again into Bobby's eyes. They were vacant. No matter what I did. He was no longer there. I crawled over to him, scratching at the ground with my nails to gain traction and pull my seemingly useless body toward him, my legs dragging behind me. Once I reached him, I curled up against him, pressing myself to him, burying my face in his silky hair. I held my hands to my ears, willing the awful high-pitched howling to stop.

Then, when I closed my mouth, it did.

. . .

DANTE CAN'T LOSE someone else. He's only just allowed himself to truly care about someone again.

I chase after Dante. He's at the nurses' station, demanding to talk to the doctor.

The woman tells him that the doctor is with Wayne right now and will speak to us after.

Then I'm holding Dante back as he rushes toward Wayne's room.

I have both arms wrapped around him from behind, and he's dragging me.

"Just wait, Dante. Let's see what the doctor says. Just wait."

When the doctor comes out, Mr. and Mrs. Clark are with us.

It's a different doctor. She has huge black eyes and silky black hair pulled back in a ponytail. She looks smart and kind at the same time. She gives us a nod.

"This is Dr. Annette Bermudez," Mrs. Clark says, introducing us. "She's the neurosurgeon who will be doing the surgery. Please tell this young man what you told us," Mrs. Clark says.

"Even with the surgery it's unlikely he will survive," the doctor says. "The brain scan last night showed some areas of gray. And the swelling in the brain, the liquid, it's not just water, it also contains blood."

We digest that for a minute and then I ask what I've been holding off asking all morning. "Who did this? What happened?"

The doctor looks at me for a long moment before she answers. "The police are asking to talk to Wayne as soon as he wakes. That's all I know."

When we sit back down, I get out my phone.

"Do you want to call your mom or do you want me to?"

"You. Please."

I think of his mom with us in Positano. She needs to be here now.

Standing, I head down the hall where Mr. and Mrs. Clark can't hear my words.

When I dial her number, it goes to her voice mail.

"This is Gia. Please call me or Dante. Dante is okay. Physically. But someone he cares about greatly is in the hospital here in San Diego and may not make it. He needs you here. I'll have a ticket waiting for you at the airport."

Then I quickly call the airline and arrange for her ticket.

Once that is done, I come back and sit down by Dante.

He turns to me.

"Wayne told me he was meeting his neighbors for dinner. That's the last time I heard from him."

I remember that fucking sketchy dude who was with his neighbor Shelby. And the weird look she gave us when we arrived at the marina yesterday morning. She knows something. I would swear to it.

Mr. Clark begins to cry. Dante and Mrs. Clark turn to him and hug and pat him.

I feel like I'm trapped in a nightmare again. The only difference this time is that Dante isn't blaming me for what happened.

"I'll be back in a while," I say. "Call me if anything changes."

10

I HEAD STRAIGHT TO THE POLICE STATION. AFTER WAITING AROUND for about an hour, I finally am met by a commander in investigations. Commander Liz Reeves.

She takes me back into her office. I follow her, trying to get a read on her.

Her standoffish air could be because she's a bitch or because she's a busy badass. I'm banking on the latter.

Her black hair falls down to her shoulders in a silky sheet and she wears a navy-blue suit that fits so well, there's no way it's not designer. Dante would be proud of my keen eye. She has on sky-high black pumps that peek out of her pant leg when she sits down.

Once she's behind her desk, she finally smiles.

"How is your friend?"

I shake my head. "Not good. He might die."

She nods, her smile gone. "Yes, that's what the doctor told me this morning."

I'm glad to hear she's keeping up on Wayne's condition, but then realize it's probably purely professional—to monitor whether the crime morphs from an assault to a homicide.

I close my eyes for a second and then pull it together.

"I'm glad you came in," she says and glances down at a notebook in front of her. "One of my investigators just spoke to Mr. Clark's parents in the hospital cafeteria and is now interviewing your friend, Dante, right?"

I nod.

"He told my investigator that Mr. Clark had mentioned he was having dinner with some neighbors at the marina?"

She looks at me. I nod. "That's all I know, too," I say, but pause.

She lifts an eyebrow. "I only met them the other day—a woman and two men, but one of the men, Bryce, struck me as ... well, fucked up. Maybe dangerous. There was something about him."

Commander Reeves holds my gaze for a few seconds longer than necessary as if she is thinking.

Then she nods. "That's helpful. I never ever discount a woman's gut instinct."

She reaches for her cell. "Do you mind?"

I shake my head.

She punches in a number.

"Make sure you talk to a guy named Bryce while you are there. See if he was at the dinner. Thanks."

Placing her phone back on the desk she looks up. "Did Mr. Clark ever mention any enemies or anything strange happening to him?"

I shake my head. "I only just met him a few weeks ago, but we have spent a lot of time together. He and my best friend, Dante, well, they just really hit it off. So, we got to know Wayne probably faster than you normally would."

She tilts her head. "Their relationship is more than platonic."

"Yes."

Something about the way she says it makes me pause.

"Do you think it might have been a hate crime?" I ask. "Because Wayne is gay?"

"We are looking at all possibilities."

"Is there anything you can tell me? Is there any hint of who did this or why?"

Standing, she heads toward the door. I stand, too. I'm done here.

"Right now, there isn't a clear-cut answer unless Wayne, Mr. Clark, wakes up and tells us what happened or we find some witnesses. I have three investigators down at the marina right now questioning everyone and looking for leads. I'm also meeting with the media in a few hours and am going to put out a request for witnesses to step forward."

I follow her down the hall. I want to argue with her, but I can't think of anything else she should be doing. It's just so frustrating.

"Is there anything I can do?" I finally say.

She hands me her card. "If you find out anything you think might be helpful if you could give me a call. That's the best thing you can do."

In the parking lot, I call Dante.

"Anything new?"

"No."

"Hey, can I have that pass, to get into the marina? I'm going to go poke around."

"Yeah. It's on the dresser in my room."

"Great."

"Gia?"

"Yep?"

"Be careful."

"What?" I'm taken aback.

"I'm not telling you anything you won't find out from his parents, but we believe someone did this to Wayne on purpose."

I nod.

"We don't believe it was a robbery. There was nothing taken from him. He had his wallet and Rolex watch still on his person. His wallet had five hundred dollars in it."

I drive home, thinking about that.

When I get home, the house is empty. I realize it's time for Rosalie to get off the school bus. I decide to surprise them both and walk to the bus stop.

I hear Nico talking to Stripper Mom before I can see them.

A row of evergreen plants hide my approach.

Then I hear Nico say something that makes me freeze.

"I may be old fashioned but I think girls should not have to learn to fight," he says.

"Oh, I couldn't agree with you more," she says. "And you're not old-fashioned. If you are, then so am I since we are the same age. I think our generation understands more than...the younger ones do. We were raised during a different time. Nobody can understand us like one of our own."

Fury rises in me for so many reasons: Nico complaining to Stripper mom about my choices. Stripper mom very subtly trying to show that she is more like Nico than I am?

I take a few deep breaths and round the corner.

"One of our own?" I say. "That doesn't sound very inclusive to me." I give a big smile.

Her distaste at seeing me lingers longer than she probably realizes before she smiles. But I'm wrapped in Nico's arms and he is hugging me and exclaiming, "God, woman I've missed you!"

Then stripper mom gets this look. "Oh, have you been gone?"

"Just for a few hours," I say, somewhat smugly.

"Oh?"

I want to slap her but I answer instead. "Wayne was attacked. He's in the hospital."

She gives Nico a strange look.

"Didn't Nico mention it?" I ask.

She frowns.

I give her a big smile and a shrug.

Then as if she is remembering how most people act, she adds, "Is he okay? Wayne?"

I shake my head. "Not really. It's touch and go."

"Oh, poor thing," she says.

But then, thank God, the bus pulls up and drowns out any other nonsense she's spewing.

In the excitement of Rosalie and Julia getting off the bus, chatting away, I completely tune her out. I crouch down and Rosalie is in my arms hugging me.

I hug her so tightly. "I missed you, Rosie."

"I missed you, too, Gia."

I hear some goodbyes being said, but I don't bother to look at our neighbor.

Then Rosalie is holding my hand on one side and Nico's on the other and we are heading home. I think Stripper Mom and her kid are somewhere behind us.

But I don't care.

11

Dante calls.

"How's Wayne?" I ask.

"They are taking him in for a scan right now. If nothing has changed, they'll do surgery within the hour."

He also said his mother arrived and went straight to the hospital to be with him.

"Can I bring you guys anything?"

"Not right now."

"Okay. Call me if they are going to do surgery and I'll head over."

Nico and I are in lounge chairs out on the patio reading when my cell rings.

Dante.

"It's a miracle," he says, breathing heavy into the phone.

I sit up straight. "He's awake?"

"No, no," Dante says, "the swelling has stopped and his brain has moved back toward where it's supposed to be."

"What?"

"His brain moved like 6 millimeters the wrong way and now it's moved back 3 millimeters."

"Okay. I'm sure that's good news. But no surgery? Thank God. And thank God the swelling has stopped."

"Gia, he has these friends who are here now. This family. A mom and dad and the two kids and they came in and they prayed over him with all of us. And, I know, you don't believe, but Gia ..."

Dante starts to cry.

"Oh, baby."

It's not that I don't believe, I say. I might believe. My mom believed. And I totally can believe that someone praying over Wayne helped. I believe that.

Before I say anything, Dante speaks again.

"The doctor says the swelling was in both the front and the back. Even though it's gone down, they say they don't know if he's going to have brain damage. They don't know when he might wake up or even if he might wake up."

"Oh, God," I say.

This could go on for a very long time.

"Dante," I say. "Are you going to come home? At least for a night? To shower and sleep?"

"I can't yet, Gia."

"Okay. What about your mom?"

"She wants to stay here with me tonight," he says. "I told her not to."

"Well, I'm making up the bed for her."

"Good. But you know how stubborn she is."

"She'll come home if you do," I say.

He's quiet for a few minutes. "If nothing changes I'll come home tomorrow night."

"Okay."

It's the best I'm going to get from him.

"Thanks, Gia."

"Sure. Call me if you need to. Otherwise I'll be there first thing in the morning."

"Love you."

"Love you, too."

Later, Rosalie is at the kitchen counter doing homework while Nico fixes dinner and I keep him company drinking a gin and tonic.

"I should probably head over to the hospital after dinner and get Mrs. Marino. I thought she could stay in the guest bedroom and we'll make up the couch for Dante if he comes home."

"I'll take care of the guest bedroom while you are gone and change the sheets and straighten up so she won't have to sleep in Dante's cologne-drenched sheets," he says.

"Thank you." I grab him and kiss him long and hard.

"Gross," Rosalie says.

"Sorry," I say. Then laugh. When did I start apologizing for kissing a man?

It's only after dinner when Rosalie is in her room playing that I bring up what happened at the bus stop. It's been bugging me. I tried to ignore it but then at dinner I realized I need to say something. But not in front of Rosie.

"I heard you complaining to the neighbor about Rosie's martial arts classes," I say casually.

He pours a drink before answering. He holds a glass for me and I shake my head no. I need my wits about me when I head to the marina soon.

"I just needed to run it by another parent," he says.

"What the fuck am I then?" I leap up.

"That's not what I meant. I meant another parent who isn't Rosalie's parent."

"Whatever," I say and tug on my leather jacket. "I'll be back later."

Well, that didn't go well, I think.

Before I go, I stop in the garage and unlock the gun safe I have hidden in a cupboard. I stick my gun in my back waistband and climb into the driver' seat of my Lincoln Navigator.

It's dark now. Several of the boats in the marina have lights on in their cabins and a few on their decks.

At the top of the stairs leading down to the docks, I wonder if these are the steps where Wayne was found. There is no sign to let me know one way or the other.

Wayne's boat is a dark hulking shape blocking the boat on the other side. When I get to it, I look it over. It looks normal.

The slip on the other side is still empty. Damn it. I should've tried to stop her when I saw her the other day. Especially now that I know she might have been with Wayne or the last one to see him before he was attacked.

A few slips down there are a few people on a boat sitting in chairs.

"Hey," I say, as I approach. "I'm friends with Wayne." I gesture toward his boat.

"Oh, man, how is he?" One woman says standing up to come over to where I am.

She's got strawberry blonde hair in a chic bob. She's wearing high-heeled slides, a silky caftan, and lots of gold. Diamond rings. Gold bracelets and layers of gold necklaces on her deeply tanned chest. She looks to be in her late forties.

"Not good," I say, shaking my head. "I'm Gia Santella."

"I'm Anissa Kennedy," she says. By the looks of her jewelry and the size of her yacht, I wonder if she's one of *those* Kennedys. "Sorry to hear that. He seems like a good guy."

"The best," I say. "I'm sure the cops already talked to you, but I was wondering if you guys were here that night?"

She shakes her head. "No, we just got back from three weeks in Cabo. We heard when we got back earlier, though."

I nod. "What about his neighbors—Shelby and Bryce and

some other guy?"

She frowns. "I don't know. We don't really talk to them much."

I pause. "Why's that?"

She shrugs. "They like to party. That's not really our scene."

"Know where they are? I saw them pulling out yesterday."

"Yeah, that's what George said: that they took off."

"George?"

She gestures to a boat on the other side of the empty slip.

"Know if he's around?" I ask, looking at the boat. It is dark.

"I think he's in the hotel bar having dinner."

"Thanks a lot," I say.

I start to leave when she calls me back. "Hey, you should probably know that the manager told us not to talk to anybody about this."

I turn back around.

"What? Why?"

"The manager here. He said something about bad publicity for the marina or something."

"What about the cops?"

"He's not going to let them into the marina again."

"That's crazy."

She shrugs.

"Why did you talk to me, then?" I ask.

"I don't care what he says. If he threatens to evict me I'll sue his ass. I've got the money to do it."

I look at her boat and the diamond rings she has and smile. "Thanks."

I think about that for a second–the manager putting the smack down on the investigation—as I walk back to the gate.

Inside the hotel, it's easy to spot George. He's the only guy at the bar alone. And the only person eating. His eyes are on the TV screen above the bar, showing the news. He's hunched over a plate of some type of seafood stew and is dipping pieces of bread into the broth.

He has gray hair and a gray beard and looks like he might be in his 70s. He wears a button down Hawaiian shirt in muted beige and khaki shorts. It's only when I sit down I notice the oxygen tank on the other side of him.

He's also drinking something amber.

"Hi," I say. "Anissa down at the marina said I might find you here. My friend Wayne is your neighbor."

Up to the point where I said Wayne's name, he'd ignored me. Now he set his fork down and turned.

"I like him."

"Yeah, what's not to like?" I say. "But he might die. Someone attacked him and I heard the manager at your marina is threatening to evict anyone who talks about it. That seems pretty strange to me."

I leave the sentence hanging for a minute. George is taking me in. He's not smiling. He's not frowning. Then he sighs.

"I wish I could tell you something. I never pass up an opportunity to disobey that fuckwad manager," he says. "But I was already below deck when it happened."

"Fuck," I say.

"Yep," he says, and turns back to his plate.

"Did you hear anything?"

He pauses, his fork lifted halfway to his mouth. He sets it back down and squints.

"They were at the barbecue area, just outside here," he points. "We can't grill on the dock you know, because of the fire hazard. But they got these grills and picnic tables."

"I saw those on the way here," I say. "That's where they had dinner?"

"I was just coming back from here when they were setting up."

"How many people were there?"

"About ten. The three bozos that are my neighbors, that gal and the two guys, and then your friend and maybe about six other people."

"Really?"

That's a lot of witnesses, I think.

"But that was it. All I saw and heard."

"Okay, thanks," I say and get up to leave.

"You should try this seafood stew while you're here. It's best thing in San Diego."

I smile. "Maybe next time."

———

I DECIDE to swing by the hospital on my way home. I know I'm avoiding talking to Nico. I'm still mad. *Run it by another parent.* Fuck him.

When I get to ICU waiting room, the first thing I do is run up to Mrs. Marino and hug her.

She's the closest thing I have to a mother now that my own is dead.

Plus, I've known her my whole life.

She draws back from the hug and smiles.

"You look amazing, Gia."

I blush and feel like I'm ten again.

"This life with Nico really suits you," she says.

I smile. I'm too embarrassed to answer.

Dante shoots Wayne's parents a glance. They don't know about my crazy life and that Nico is in witness protection.

His mom knows everything. She knows I've killed. She knows the things I've seen and done.

And she still loves me.

I lean in and hug her again. "I've missed you."

She pats my back.

"You are like my own child, Gia," she says. "I'm always here for you. Don't you ever forget that."

I try not to cry as I pull back.

Then I go over to Wayne's parents.

"I was so happy to hear the swelling went down," I say.

Mrs. Clark smiles. "My boy is a fighter. He's survived worse than this."

I smile back. "I've heard."

Mr. Clark nudges her. She turns to him. "Oh, yes, we were just about to go find some food. Neither one of us has been able to eat a darn thing since we got here. But now we're both starving!"

"That sounds lovely," Dante's mother says.

"We're going to go have a proper meal down in the cafeteria," she says. "Would you care to join us?"

Mrs. Marino smiles. "If you don't think I'd be a third wheel?"

"Oh, honey, when you've been married as long as we have, we welcome a third wheel."

I laugh.

She turns to us. "Dante?"

Dante just smiles. "No, but thank you."

"Gia?"

"Thanks, I already had dinner."

We watch as the three of them head down the hall to the elevator.

Dante hiccups and I look over at him. His eyes are red. I lean in. He smells like booze.

"Are you drunk?"

"Mr. Clark and I have been drinking."

His words are slurred. He lifts the flap of his black leather messenger bag and I see the tops of two bottles. "Mr. Clark brought it from home. We've been drinking all day."

"Well, I don't blame you. Give me a swig," I say.

He hands me the bottle and I tip it back. I wipe my mouth when I'm done.

"Damn, that's good. What is it?"

"Moonshine? Not sure," he says. "It's strong as fuck, though."

We both start to laugh. But his laughter sounds like he's strangling and then comes to an abrupt halt.

I look over at Dante.

He has tears running down his cheeks.

"Gia," he says. "I love Wayne."

"I know, honey." I lean over and hug him.

After a few seconds, he stops crying and we sit back.

"Gimme another swig," I say.

We both down some more. My throat burns with the heat and my belly is suddenly very warm. I'm not even sure I can drive home without waiting a while. Holy shit.

I lean back and look over at Dante, who is also slumped in his chair.

"Dante, do you think this is it?"

He shoots a surprised glance at me so I quickly keep talking.

"Do you think we've grown up? Do you think..." I choke on the words but force them out, "that we've actually found true love again?"

He nods, fighting his own tears.

"I do, Gia," He says. "That's why I can't let him go."

"He's a fighter," I say. "The doctors are shocked he's still alive now. Remember what he told us about having all those lives? Like his mom mentioned? Like getting trapped in the refrigerator and stuff?"

Dante nods.

"He's not going anywhere."

I hope I'm right.

12

When I get home, Nico is sound asleep.

Of course, he is.

Like an argument with me would keep him up? Shit, he's sleeping like a fucking baby even though I ran out of the house pissed off at him.

I sigh.

Maybe I was over-reacting? But then again, maybe not.

I slip into bed and instantly fall asleep because the next thing I remember is waking to sun streaming through our curtains.

Nico is peeking through our cracked bedroom door.

"Sorry, I didn't mean to wake you."

I frown and sit up. "It's fine. I need to get up anyway."

I glance at the clock. I missed saying goodbye to Rosalie before school. Damn it.

"You hungry?"

I nod, too sleepy to argue or be angry.

He pushes the door in and has a tray. It has eggs and cheese on a tortilla with beans and cilantro and sour cream. Yum. With coffee. And a flower.

He brings it to me.

I sigh. I don't want to fight with him. I don't have the energy.

"I want to apologize. You are more of a parent than me."

I frown. "That's not true."

"I know you don't like Gloria. So, I will not share our private family business with her ever again. Out of respect for you."

But then he growls at me. Like it literally sounds like a growl.

"But I don't like jealous women, Gia. You don't need to be jealous and I expect you to act accordingly."

I let him do his big bad bear impression for his ego and nod meekly.

Then, I move the tray aside. "Good. Now, that we've cleared all that up, let's make up."

He laughs. "You are insatiable."

"Whatever. I don't hear you complaining. Ever."

I'm reaching for him, but he's frowning.

"What? Don't tell me you're not in the mood," I say reaching for him. "Because this tells me differently."

"It's not that. It's that I am so much older. What if my desire one day doesn't match yours."

"Whatever," I say again. "We'll deal with it then. There's these little blue pills…"

He laughs and then leans down to kiss me. I forget about everything else, including why I was angry.

The day passes quickly and soon Rosalie is home.

I sit at the counter with her as she does homework.

Dante had called earlier and I'd somehow talked him, his mother, and Wayne's parents into coming home for a few hours. At least to eat and sleep.

Nico just left for the hospital to collect them all.

After Nico fed them all dinner, Wayne's parents would sleep at Wayne's in the guest room.

Dante was going to sleep in Wayne's bed. Mrs. Clark had insisted.

"We'd like the company," she'd told him.

Dante's mother would stay with us.

Then we would all wake early and head to the hospital the next morning.

I didn't tell them that as soon as everyone went to bed, I was heading to the marina again. When I'd called the commander earlier, she'd said they didn't have anything new. When I'd asked if she'd spoken to Shelby, she said they were still trying to locate the people Wayne had been with that night.

So as soon as its dark and everyone has turned in, I'm heading to the marina.

I'm going to find out what the fuck happened to Wayne.

13

THE FIRST THING EVERYONE DOES WHEN THEY GET HOME IS TAKE turns in the shower. Dante takes Wayne's parents next door while Dante's mother uses our bathroom.

When everyone is clean and back at our house, we head out to the patio and have drinks and chips and salsa.

"This is beautiful," Mrs. Clark says. "It's like a little oasis. A little haven."

"Totally," I say. "I spend as much time as I can here."

Rosalie sits on Mrs. Marino's lap. She's the closest thing that girl has to a grandmother. Mrs. Marino is brushing her hair, getting it ready for braiding.

"Thank you for taking us in like this, making us part of your family," Mrs. Clark says.

I smile and look toward the house where Dante is helping Nico make dinner. "I have a feeling that we probably all are going to be family."

She smiles and then swallows and looks away.

We are all thinking the same thing—if Wayne makes it through this.

"Any change today?" I ask.

"Nothing," Mr. Clark says.

I immediately want to change the subject.

"Tell us about Wayne's nine lives," I say. It was all I needed to say. They both launch into funny stories about how Wayne survived crazy things over his life.

By the time they finish, Nico and Dante have brought dinner out.

After dessert and after-dinner drinks, Mr. and Mrs. Clark plead that they are exhausted and Dante leaves with them. His mother walks them to the door and then also goes to bed.

Rosalie was put to bed a while ago.

Once the front door closes, I turn to Nico.

I'd told him my plans earlier.

"I'm leaving now."

"Be careful," he says.

"I will."

14

When I first arrive at the marina, I head to the hotel bar.

George nods when I sat down.

"I was hoping you'd come back," he says.

"Oh, yeah, why's that? The seafood stew?"

"Nah. They only have that on Tuesdays. Anissa said she heard some people talking. Shelby is coming back tonight. I know you wanted to talk to her."

"Buy this man another drink on me," I tell the bartender.

I pay for his dinner, too, and then leave. I sit in my car until dark. I text Nico and tell him I'm going to be later than I thought.

And then I venture out to the picnic area between the marina and the hotel. It's a grassy area with grills and picnic tables above the marina. It gives me a good view of the row where Wayne's boat is docked. Shelby's boat slip is empty.

I wait until I see the majority of the lights on the boats go out.

I watch the lights on George's boat go out, as well.

And still I wait. I sit in my dark clothes—black jeans, black jacket—and wait, hoping I blend into the night.

Then, under cover of darkness, I see a boat coming down the row and pull into the empty slip. Shelby.

I wait ten minutes and then I slip into the marina using the key card Wayne gave Dante and make sure the gate doesn't clank loudly when it closes behind me. It's past midnight.

I pass Wayne's boat and carefully poke my head around the side to where Shelby's boat is.

She's still tying up the boat to the dock.

I come around the front.

"Where's your friends?" I say.

She jumps. "Jesus Christ, you scared the shit out of me."

When she realizes it's me, she scowls.

"Hey," I say, walking closer. "Heard Wayne was with you guys the night he was attacked."

"I don't know nothing about that," she says, but looks away.

"You don't know anything about him being with you or you don't know anything about him being attacked?"

She glares at me. "About the attack," she says irritably. She finishes tying up the boat and then stands there with her arms crossed.

"Why don't we start with him being with you and we'll go from there," I say.

"What do you want to know? We had dinner. He drank too much. Next thing I know he's at the bottom of the stairs."

"He doesn't drink."

She raises an eyebrow. "That's not what I saw."

"You saw him drinking? Alcohol?"

She frowns. "Well, no, but he was drunk."

"That would be very strange."

"Shit happens," she says.

"Let's back up. Tell me about when you first saw him that day."

He was working on his boat, she says. He was doing some

paint touch up and then he joined a bunch of them up at the picnic area for a barbecue.

"He brought some wine. Even though he doesn't drink," she says in a snotty voice.

"Yeah. He always brings wine. Go on."

"He had some fish from the grill. I remember that."

"Do you remember seeing him drinking alcohol?"

She shakes her head.

"Then what?"

"Some of us went into the hotel club to dance. He didn't come. Next thing I know the cops and ambulance are coming."

She won't meet my eyes.

"You know what happened to him, don't you?" I say. "You know who hit him. I can tell. You better fucking speak up."

I'm leaning in her face. She puts her foot out and pushes the boat away from me before she speaks.

"Fuck you."

I'm about to hop on her boat when I hear a voice behind me.

"Excuse me? Shelby? Is this woman bothering you?"

I turn. I see a guy in a jacket and ball cap pulled low on the dock.

"Why yes, Tyler. She is. Asking questions about Wayne. I told her I couldn't talk to her. That you said so."

The guy is coming closer.

"You must be the manager who is trying to interfere with a police investigation," I say.

He stops dead. "You a cop?"

"You can't tell people not to talk about a crime," I say.

His eyes narrow. "You ain't no cop. Get out of here before I call the police. You're trespassing."

I wait, wondering what he's going to do. He reaches for his phone and punches in three times. Probably 911.

"It's pretty strange that you don't want this crime solved. It seems like having it solved would be better for business. Covering it up, well, you know it's going to get out one way or the other. And then you're even more fucked."

"Fuck you," he says. And then, "I'd like to report a trespasser."

I brush past him.

I can't hear the rest of what he says. I am up the stairs and in my car.

As I drive away, I see a squad car heading toward the parking lot.

What the fuck?

I will call Commander Reeves in the morning. Something is really wrong here.

———

THE NEXT MORNING, I call the commander as soon as I wake.

"I was at the marina last night," I begin.

"So, I heard. First thing. Trespassing. A woman who fits your description."

"I'm sure there are lots of Italian-American women with dark hair around here."

She laughs.

"You can't go into the marina. You're not a member."

"Fine. Let me tell you what I think."

I tell her about how hinky Shelby was acting.

"We heard she was back and I sent an investigator to talk to her this morning."

"I don't buy a word she says. She said Wayne was drinking. He doesn't drink."

"You know this?"

"Yes."

"People slip up," she says.

I sigh. "Maybe. But even if he was drinking and say, fell, he wouldn't have injuries on the front and back of his head and a black eye, do you agree?"

"We do think he was attacked."

"And then she leaves right away?"

"We're questioning her."

I keep trying to convince her that Shelby knows what happened but she keeps putting me off saying it's an open investigation, blah blah.

Finally, I say, "Okay. Well, I'm going to put my trust in you doing the best job you can on this."

"I always do," she says.

I hang up not sure if I dislike her or want to be best friends.

I pad into the kitchen in bare feet and a short robe.

Nico is leaning over Rosalie at the kitchen bar. She's staring straight ahead.

I can tell she's pissed.

He glances at me over her head and shakes his head.

Shit.

I pull out the stool beside her and sit down.

"Morning, Rosie."

She glares at me. Django comes up and licks my hand. At least someone around here likes me.

"What did I do?" I ask.

With a huff, she turns away from me.

Nico straightens and goes behind the bar to grab me a cup of coffee from the moka pot on the stove.

"Rosie says she hates school. That the girls there are mean and that she wants to go to the hospital with us today instead."

I think about that for a few seconds before I answer.

I take a sip of my coffee and then another.

"What do you think?" Nico asks.

"Rosie," I say leaning so I can see her face. "I get you want to go see Wayne. And I think you have a right to that. But I want you to know that when I saw him like that it was pretty upsetting."

She turns to me, still frowning. At least she is listening.

"It does look like he's sleeping but he also has bandages all over his head and a lot of tubes on his body connecting him to the machines that are helping him right now."

"I know. I've watched Grey's Anatomy," she says indignantly.

"I understand that, but this is someone you care about so it might be different."

"I want to see him." Her voice is steel.

I look at Nico. He shrugs.

"How about this? I don't want you to miss school or get behind, so here's what I think. As soon as you get off the bus this afternoon we will all go to the hospital together. And maybe, just maybe, Wayne will be awake by then."

She whirls. "He might?"

I shrug. "He might. Nobody knows. But he might not ever wake up, too."

I had to say it. Especially after I saw her hopes get up.

"Maybe if I talk to him he'll want to wake up," she says.

I smile. "You know, you might be right."

She hops off the stool and says over her shoulder, "I'm going to miss the bus if we don't leave right now."

Nico rolls his eyes, but he is smiling.

"Coming!"

After they walk out, I realize that there is a whole different issue we still need to deal with—the mean girls at school.

Tonight.

When Nico comes back from the bus stop, he is smiling and wraps me in a hug.

"Thank you for talking her off the ledge."

"You would have eventually done it, too."

"I said no to the hospital visit," he says.

"Oh. Shit, did I overstep? Undermine what you said?"

"I put you on the spot and asked what you thought, so no."

"Good."

"And the way you explained it made sense to me. She does have a right to see him. Especially if he does die."

I nod and suddenly choke up. I've been holding my feelings back. Not only would I grieve Wayne's death for me, I would grieve it for Dante and Rosalie. That's too much.

"He better wake up," I say.

Nico doesn't answer.

————

I CALL Dante to tell him that we are bringing Rosie there in the afternoon.

He says nothing has changed.

He sounds dejected.

"It's still early, right?" I ask.

He doesn't answer.

"See you soon," I say. "Call me if you need me to bring anything."

The day passes quickly. It's getting close to time to get ready to get Rosie and head to the hospital.

Nico is in his office doing whatever day trading shit he does.

I'm out on the patio listening to my Italian language tapes when Nico comes out in a hurry. His face is white.

He's holding his phone.

My heart sinks. Wayne is dead.

But it's not Wayne.

"The school called," he says. "Rosalie..." He closes his eyes.

I'm instantly up and at his side. "What?" I shake him. "Is she okay?"

"She is okay. But she ... well... she wouldn't come out of the bathroom stall. They had to break the door down."

"Oh, my God." I grab my phone off the patio table. "Let's go."

———

THE PRINCIPAL IS YOUNG. Probably my age. A redhead with a round face and blue blazer.

She meets us at the door to her office. "Rosalie is in the nurse's office lying down. She won't talk to us. I don't know what to do."

"It's okay," Nico says. "A close family friend is in the hospital very ill and she is worried."

The principal looks relieved to hear there might be a reason for all of this. But her next words make me freeze.

"Her teachers say she is disrupting the whole class. She's talking out of turn and saying things that are, quite frankly, disturbing to the other students. And the teacher."

"Like what?" I say.

The principal looks extremely uncomfortable and it makes my blood run cold.

"Like what?" I repeat.

The woman exhales loudly. "They were talking about religious ceremonies and she blurted out something like 'everyone will die anyway. They always do.'"

I close my eyes and shake my head. Nico put his arm around me.

But the principal isn't done.

"And then there is the matter of her art work."

My eyes fly open. Shit. I remember the art she showed me in her room. Morbid as fuck. But it's art. Who cares?

The woman turns toward her office. "I think I should just show you."

We file into her office. Nico has his arm around me. I feel weak and he is holding me up.

The principal hands us a stack of papers.

Nico and I flip through them. I feel like I'm going to vomit.

I open my mouth to speak but nothing comes out.

They are horrific nightmare scenes. Even worse than the ones she shared with me. Of violence and blood. Dead bodies that are disemboweled. I can't breathe. Nico's grip on my shoulder tightens.

I remember what Rosie said about not wanting anyone to see her pictures because they might think she's a "freak."

I turn to the principal. "Did she turn these pictures in or show them to anyone?

The woman squirms a little. "Well, no, but they were in her folder. When her teacher was looking for an assignment, she found them."

I can feel my face harden. I know not to open my mouth or I'll fuck everything up. But I'm furious. Those pictures were only for Rosie. Nobody else. And now she's being punished for it. She's being ostracized for drawings that are most likely a form of therapy for her.

"She has been through a lot," Nico says. "She has not had it easy. Her mother was murdered."

He leaves it at that.

The principal's face softens but then she purses her lips together. I'm afraid of what she's going to say next. And I'm right to be.

"I think before she returns to school you might want to consider having her see a therapist," she says. "We actually think that this needs to happen before she comes back to school."

I open my eyes. "You think? Or you require this?"

She winces. "We're going to need a note."

I want to be angry. I want to argue with the woman. But I

can't. Rosalie needs help. I don't know how I didn't see it until now.

The principal takes us into the nurses' office. Rosalie is in a back corner lying on a bed behind a curtain. She is curled up and sound asleep. My heart breaks seeing her. I sit on the bed and brush back her hair from her face. Her eyes fly open and she jumps up and shouts. I just take her in my arms and hold her tight.

"It's going to be okay, baby, it's going to be okay."

We don't talk on the way home.

As we pull into the garage, Rosie starts to scream. Like scream bloody murder and kick the back of the seat with her feet.

"I want to see Wayne! I want to see Wayne!"

I look at Nico and he shakes his head.

"We'll go later," I say.

She is now wailing and pounding the seat with her fists and still kicking.

I whirl around. "We will only go later if you stop that nonsense and go in the house." I am not proud that I use my bitchiest voice.

Surprisingly she stops and opens the door.

Once we are inside the house, she is subdued. Nico takes her by the hand and leads her to the bedroom. Django follows them. I let him do it alone. I will talk to her later. This is his time.

When he comes out, he looks ten years older.

He sits and puts his head in his hands. "I just wanted her to have a normal life, Gia."

I put my arm around him. "I know."

15

Nico is holding Rosie's hand as we enter the hospital.

He leans down. "Are you sure?" he asks her.

She nods solemnly.

I wonder about the wisdom of having her see Wayne after what happened at school earlier, but Nico seems to think it's the best thing to do. I just don't know.

When we step out of the elevator into the ICU floor, Rosie sees Dante in the family waiting room. She lets go of Nico's hand and races over to him, throwing herself in his arms.

Wayne's parents sit nearby. His mother is knitting and his father is reading on an iPad. Dante's mother is watching Rosie and Dante and smiling.

After Dante extracts himself from her death grip he looks over at me and bursts into tears.

I'm horrified. We're too late. But he is smiling. And his mother was smiling when we got here?

"He blinked his eyes. He opened his eyes for a few seconds and blinked."

"Wow," I say. "That's great news, right?"

I'm not positive. I remember when a friend's sister-in-law

was in a coma and started opening her eyes and mumbling things and while everyone was ecstatic about it, it really only spelled the end for her. I guess shit like that can happen before they die.

"I'll let Mrs. Clark explain. She spoke to the doctor," Dante says.

Mrs. Clark is smiling. She sets down her knitting. "The doctor says that the scan this morning showed his brain is back in the right place, the swelling is gone, the fluid is gone and there is some strange brain activity they didn't expect."

"Really? Like what?"

"There are areas that were gray so they were worried about brain damage there, but it seems like some other areas of the brain are now lighting up. I don't really know how to explain it other than that and to say that the doctor seems to think all of this is really good news."

"Wow."

Rosalie is standing up, holding Dante's hand.

"Can I see him? Please?" she asks. He doesn't answer just looks at me.

Not missing a beat, Rosalie lets go of his hand and is front of Wayne's parents.

She folds her arms across her chest. "I need to see him."

Mrs. Clark looks over at me and I nod. I can't even say how grateful I am that she looks to me as Rosie's mom, like I have the final say. It brings tears to my eyes.

Then she smiles at Rosie. "Of course." She stands. "I'll take you to see him right now."

———

Rosalie comes back from seeing Wayne a half hour later looking very solemn.

She runs to her dad and buries her face in his shirt. He hugs her and strokes her hair and looks at me.

Mrs. Clark says in a firm voice. "It's hard to see him like that, isn't it Rosie?"

She nods, but keeps her face buried.

"It's hard for me, too, but I just have this feeling that everything is going to be okay. Do you know why?"

Rosalie shakes her head. Then she draws back and looks at Mrs. Clark.

"Come over here," Mrs. Clark says patting the seat beside her. "And I'll tell you why. It has to do with my son having nine lives. I'll tell you what? That kid has survived the craziest things in his life..."

Rosie laughs. "He's not a kid. He's a grown man."

"True. But come over here and sit and I'll tell you some of the crazy scrapes he's gotten himself into over the years."

Rosalie plops down beside her and I smile.

Nico takes my arm. "Let's go see him."

Inside the room, we stand over Wayne. Whatever his mother saw that gave her hope is not apparent. He looks awful. His skin looks green and his head is still full of bandages and the tubes ... I can't stay very long.

When I come back to the family waiting room, however, I smile at Rosie.

She is smiling at what Mrs. Clark is telling her.

For the first time, I think that it was a good idea to bring Rosie here today.

When we leave, Dante follows us out.

"What did you find out at the marina?" he says in a low voice. Nico and Rosie are walking some ways ahead of us.

I stop. "Not much. They called the cops on me."

"What?"

I explain and tell him that Shelby is hiding something.

"But I'm going back."

"I'll come"

"Okay. Tomorrow night?" I say.

Dante nods. "Yes."

"Does that mean you're coming home?"

He shrugs. "I don't know."

Wayne's parents are using their son's car to go back and forth to the hospital. They are going to give Dante's mother a ride, as well. She has her own key and comes home after I'm asleep and then is gone again when I wake.

But Dante insists on sleeping at the hospital in case Wayne wakes. He's going to keep sleeping in a chair next to Wayne's bed, he says.

"Oh, Dante."

I don't know what else to say.

"If I didn't stay, then you know Wayne's parents would be there. I need to stay there. Someone needs to be there."

I nod. He's right. I don't blame him at all.

I hug him goodbye. "Call me if anything changes."

It's the new way of saying goodbye.

16

WHEN I WAKE THE NEXT MORNING I'M RELIEVED THAT I HAVEN'T heard from Dante.

No news is good news.

Rosie is in the kitchen, petting Django, who is sprawled on his back, his feet comically in the air so she can scratch his belly.

When I see her, I remember that we still have to figure out the school situation. Therapy. Fuck.

Rosie stands. She's already dressed.

"I'm going to ask Julia to come over today," she says.

I pause. Nico isn't in the kitchen. "Did your dad say it's okay?"

"Yes."

"Okay." I smile tightly.

Rosie needs her friends. And I do like Julia. Even if I don't like her mother. And there is no way in hell I'll let Rosalie go over there to see her friend. So, it's our house.

Last night when we came home Nico and I went out on the patio for a drink after Rosie went to bed. We could hear music and giggling from the Stripper's yard.

I bring that up now.

"Does anyone else live at Julia's house besides her mother?" I ask, trying to sound innocent. I want to know because if there is a man there I'm even more determined not to have Rosalie go over there. I just don't trust Gloria. And I wouldn't trust anyone she dated. I know I'm paranoid. But God knows I've seen the worst of people in my life.

Rosie frowns. "Yes. Why?"

"I just heard voices."

"Oh," Rosalie says. "She has a boyfriend. He sometimes has a sleep over, Julia says."

"Oh, okay." Again, I try to keep my voice nonchalant.

"Should I call Julia now and tell her to come over?"

I look at the time and get an idea.

"Well, she's in school right now and probably wouldn't be able to even ask her mom. Why don't I go ask her mom?"

Julia is the only friend Rosalie has. I will make peace with the mother just for her sake.

The woman is probably lonely. I'm glad to hear she has a boyfriend. Even if it means Rosalie can't go over there for play dates.

I'm too jaded and aware of the monsters in the world not to be suspicious of any man dating a single mom with young kids. It's sad but true.

While Nico and Rosalie play video games that afternoon, I grab a bottle of chilled Limoncello and a package of biscotti and head next door. I don't tell them I'm leaving.

The house next door has pretty pots of flowers near the door. I ring the doorbell. After a while, Gloria comes and opens it. She doesn't seem surprised to see me.

She's wearing short shorts and a tight, low-cut tank top. I have to admit for an older woman, she's got a great body. She doesn't look Nico's age.

"Come in," she says. "That looks like it's going to hit the spot. I've had a shitty day. Let's head to the backyard."

I follow her through an immaculate house, glancing around quickly. She has a big cushiony couch and a giant arrangement of fresh flowers on the coffee table in front of it. We pass through the kitchen to large French doors leading to the backyard. The kitchen has a giant marble island. Everything is gleaming. The stove is pristine. I wonder if she cooks. Or, looking at her tiny backside, eats? She is grabbing small glasses out of a cupboard for the Limoncello.

The home, from what I can see, is beautiful. But it's almost too perfect. Sterile. I give one last glance around before I follow her outside. Then it hits me. There are no family photos. There is also nothing personal. Nothing that would give a clue to who lives there. It's almost as if it is staged by a real estate agent to be generic.

It's so sterile. I'd expect to see pictures of her dead son at the very least. But then again, maybe that's too painful. Maybe school pictures of Julia?

The backyard is mostly grass. There is a grape arbor over a patio connected to the house. We sit at a table underneath facing the yard. The wall on her side is bordered with flower beds.

"Your flowers are beautiful," I say.

"Thanks," she says. "It's about the only domestic bone I have in my body. I have a green thumb."

"Really?" I say, surprised. "Your house is immaculate."

"Oh that," she says, flailing one hand. "That's just surface clean."

She laughs. "All the dirt is hidden or swept under the rug, so they say."

I think about that. It's an odd statement.

I pour us some of the icy vodka-lemon mix and break open the bag of biscotti.

"I like to dip my cookie in the Limoncello. It's an Italian thing. You get crumbs in your drink, but it tastes damn good."

She nods. "I'll give a try."

She reaches for a biscotti and dips it in the Limoncello before she takes a bite.

Closing her eyes, she murmurs her approval. "Oh, yeah. That's definitely the right way to do it. You Italians are on to something."

I nod. I hate that I sort of like her right now.

"I don't know if you heard, but Rosalie is having a tough time at school," I say.

Gloria frowns. "Julia said she had to go home, but she didn't really say why."

"I think the kids at school are being little assholes to Rosalie," I say.

She doesn't flinch at the word.

"Children can be so cruel," she says.

For some reason, she doesn't meet my eyes. I'm wondering if people were mean to her son. The dead one.

"I'm really grateful that Rosalie has Julia for a friend."

She looks at me in surprise. But doesn't speak so I continue.

"Would it be okay for Julia to come over after school today? I know Rosie would love to have her. I can feed her dinner and then walk her back home by about seven?"

Gloria looks at me and there is something unnerving about her look. Is it because the invitation is only for her child? I don't know.

"How is Wayne?" she asks.

I'm a little taken aback by the change of subject. And she still hasn't said it's okay for Julia to come over.

"There's some promising signs. I think he blinked or something. And they didn't have to do surgery like they thought. The swelling is down. But the doctors say whether he has brain damage or even wakes up is still up in the air."

Her nose crinkles. "That's too bad."

But the way she says it makes me think she could give a shit.

An awkward silence grows between us. We've polished off half the Limoncello bottle and I'm feeling no pain. That happens with Limoncello. It tastes so sweet and you forget it's basically vodka spiked with lemon and sugar.

I stand. "Can I use your bathroom?"

She looks startled. I file that away. Maybe it's rude in San Diego to use someone's bathroom. I giggle at the thought.

Finally, she stands. "I'll show you where it is."

That's weird.

I follow her down a hall. There are two doors open. I see an office and Julia's room full of girly things. A door on the other side has a padlock. That's really weird. And then there's the bathroom.

She turns on the light for me.

I go in and close the door listening to see if she is walking away. I don't hear a thing. Is she waiting right outside? Is she listening?

I use the bathroom, wash my hands and come out. She's still standing there, leaning against the wall.

"I'll walk you out," she says.

She does not like me in her house unsupervised, does she?

I follow her to the front door.

She doesn't offer to give me the rest of the Limoncello and I don't go back to grab the bottle. It was a gift.

"Do you want me to swing by and grab Julia after school or do you want to drop her off?" I ask.

She looks at a watch, some exercise tracker black thing.

"I'll bring her by."

"Cool."

Another awkward silence and then she closes the door.

Well, mission accomplished.

We'll never be friends. But at least we can be civil to each other for the girls' sakes.

That's enough.

On the walk home, I take out my phone.

I missed a dozen calls. Dante. Nico. Rosalie.

I dial Nico first. "Is everything okay?"

My heart is racing.

"Yes. Where were you?"

I appreciate how he answered my question before he scolded me.

"I'm sorry, I was at the neighbors offering a peace treaty for the sake of Rosie's friendship with her kid. I'm almost there."

"Wayne woke up."

My body sags in relief.

"Thank God." But then I remember what the doctor said. "Is he...? You know? Normal?"

"I don't know. Dante's with him now."

Then I'm in our front door. Nico is at the bar counter with Rosalie.

I hang up. "Sorry I didn't let you know where I was," I say kissing her head.

She glares at me. "Don't do that again. I was worried, Gia."

"Oh, honey. You're right. I won't leave again without telling you."

I grab my keys and then when I realize I can't drive, I pause.

Nico looks at me. "I was going to go the hospital," I say, "but...I've been drinking."

He punches in something on his phone.

"Your car is here in five minutes."

"Thanks," I kiss him and then head back outside.

At the hospital, I rush to the family waiting room. Dante is there with his mother. Wayne's parents must be in with him.

"How is he?"

Dante shakes his head. "He can't really talk, but the doctors said that's normal for right now."

"Did he recognize you?" I ask.

Dante grins. "Yes. He reached for me. And smiled."

"Oh, thank God."

That was what I was most worried about.

"That's great news."

"The best."

Even if there was some brain damage, Wayne knew who Dante was and smiled.

After about an hour, Wayne's parents come out.

"Wayne is napping," Mrs. Clark said to Dante. "We just met with the doctor and they are going to do a series of tests when he wakes again. If he passes one test, they'll do another and so on. Then he will go to occupational therapy. He might have to relearn some things. They are going to transfer him to another wing tomorrow."

I smile. "You were right Mrs. Clark. He does have nine lives."

She smiles. "My boy is a fighter."

Mr. Clark grins. "He sure is."

I turn to Dante's mother. "I'm going to head home now. Want to come with me? Have some dinner? Maybe some wine?"

She stands but then looks at Dante. "Will you come home tonight, too, honey? Just one night in a real bed?"

He looks like he might but then he says. "I'm going to stay until Wayne wakes up again and then I'll probably come home too, and bring Mr. and Mrs. Clark with me. I think it's time."

"Oh, please," Mrs. Clark says, "call me Cheryl. And call him John."

Dante grins. "Of course."

NICO BREAKS into his most expensive stash of Champagne and we toast Wayne out on the patio before dinner.

It's a very late dinner, nearly nine o'clock.

Everyone is there except Wayne of course.

Julia had already gone home by the time I got back from the hospital. Nico said the girls played video games for hours. Lots of girlish screams and laughter. I'm glad.

As he pours the champagne, Nico even gives Rosie a tiny splash in a glass. She takes a sip and wrinkles her nose.

Dante and Nico bring out a special dinner—a massive plate of paella with fresh seafood. It has massive shrimp, scallops, oysters, mussels, and clams. And the most melt in your mouth saffron rice.

Then for dessert, Dante's mom makes homemade brownies.

And we have lots of wine.

We are all a little tipsy and telling stories and laughing when I realize it's nearly midnight.

People are starting to yawn.

Rosie is in her dad's lap fighting sleep, so I stand. "Come on, Rosie, I'll tuck you in."

She yawns stands. "I'm not a baby. I don't need to be tucked in."

I nod. "Right. I'll walk you to your room, then."

She rolls her eyes.

But Dante gets the hint and stands, looking at Cheryl and John. "Ready?"

He holds out his arm for Cheryl. She stands and grasps it. "You are such a gentleman!"

"Why don't we all plan on heading to the hospital tomorrow around nine?" I say. "I can fit everyone in the Lincoln. Sound good?"

When I crawl into bed after cleaning up, Nico is snoring beside me. I curl up against him and nearly cry with happiness.

Wayne is awake. My family is healthy and safe. Although I've been away from the family I created in San Francisco—my close friends: Darling, Kato, Danny—I have a family here, too.

I loved tonight more than I could say. It felt like one big happy family. I didn't realize until now just how much I've missed that.

17

THE NEXT DAY, NICO AND I TAKE ROSALIE TO HER FIRST THERAPY appointment.

She refuses to talk. The therapist comes out and says that Rosie sat there with her arms crossed over her chest the entire time. Glaring.

Nico and I exchange looks, but don't say anything.

The therapist, a chic woman dressed all in black with knee-high black boots and black hair streaked silver gray, shrugs.

"Call me if she decides she wants to talk."

She hands me her business card. It's all black with white letters that say her name—Taloo Carrillo—and her cell number.

On the drive home, Rosalie pouts.

"I don't need therapy."

"Everyone needs therapy," I say.

She scowls.

"Well, I don't."

"Your teacher seems to think you do."

"Whatever. She doesn't know me or my life."

"True," Nico says.

"Just because I express myself through my art doesn't mean I'm a weirdo."

I shoot a glance at her. Her lower lip is wobbling. She's going to cry.

"Of course, you're not a weirdo," I say.

She doesn't answer. She just looks out the window.

My heart breaks. She's always going to be different. She's always going to be "other." There is no other option. How can she not? She's seen those she loved murdered in front of her. She lost her innocence a long time ago. Who is the school to say she needs therapy because she is drawing macabre pictures? Maybe that is her therapy?

The more I think about it, the more indignant I get.

And then I remember how the girls at school are little assholes to her anyway.

I need to talk to Nico about other options besides that school.

I only hope he is opened minded to it, since he's so adamant about trying to give her a "normal" childhood.

He needs to realize that ship sailed long ago.

———

THAT NIGHT ROSALIE wakes us with bloodcurdling screams. We both rush into her bedroom. She is sitting up in bed, wild-eyed, sweating, and shaking.

"What is it?" I ask looking around her room. Django, on the foot of her bed, yawns.

"I had a bad dream."

I sink onto her bed and reach for her hand.

"The person who tried to kill Wayne wants to kill me, too."

I hug her. I look at Nico's face over her head. He's wincing. I wait for him to answer her. When he doesn't, I say, "You don't need to worry about that, honey."

"I'm scared, Gia."

"I know. But what happened to Wayne had nothing to do with you."

"But someone could do that to me. If someone did that to Wayne, who is good and nice, it could happen to me. Or you. Or Daddy."

I don't know what to say. I just hug her tighter.

Finally, Nico speaks. "We would never let that happen to you. Besides, you have Django to protect you."

"But he's not with me all the time, Daddy. What about when I can't have him with me?"

She's right.

Then I say something spontaneously.

"I'll teach you to shoot a gun Rosalie. So, you know how to defend yourself."

"Yes!" She sits up straight. "Yes, please."

Nico's head jerks my way.

"Absolutely not. No way in hell." He is angry.

"Why not, Nico? Boys her age in some places learn how to shoot. They learn gun safety. Did you know they used to teach it in school?"

His face is pure fury.

"Can I please speak to you in the hall?"

I stand but Rosalie holds tight to my hand. "Can I sleep in your room?"

"Of course," I say.

She holds my hand and follows us back to our room. She climbs into the big bed right between us and instantly falls asleep. Django follows us and curls up on the floor by my side.

I can feel that Nico is awake and tense on the other side of me. He's pissed. Maybe angrier than I've seen him.

I don't care.

In the morning, we both rise early. Rosie stays asleep in the bed. Out in the kitchen, Nico stomps around making coffee. I sit at the bar counter and try to ignore him.

Despite his anger, he places a cup of coffee in front of me. We both drink a cup before he speaks.

"I do not want Rosalie to learn how to shoot a gun."

"Yeah, I got that," I say coolly. "But I'm going to teach her."

He grows tense. His eyes bore through me. "I am her father."

"Whatever," I yawn. "We share joint custody, remember. I'll just teach her during the times she's in my custody."

He rolls his eyes. "That's absurd. We live together. There is no custody, right now."

"She's seen people murdered in front of her, Nico," I say. "More than once. She needs to be able to defend herself. And she needs the confidence that she can defend herself. How do you think it would feel to be 90 pounds and unable to physically defend yourself? You have no idea, do you?"

He glares.

"She's a smart girl. She'll be careful. She's not going to look at guns as toys. Trust her," I say. "Boys learn this shit at her age. Then they go hunting. How is this different?"

"She's not shooting deer. We don't live in the woods. We live in the city."

"Whatever."

He hates when I say that. Which is why I say it a lot when we argue.

I sense her behind me before she speaks.

"Gia is right. I'm smart," she says. "I will be very careful, Daddy. I promise."

He looks at me and bites the inside of his lip instead of answering.

Then he turns on his heel and leaves, slamming the garage door behind him.

I hear the engine of his car start up and then hear it drive down the street.

Whatever.

18

THAT NIGHT, AFTER NICO AND I SPENT THE DAY AVOIDING EACH other—in a stalemate with him in his office and me on the patio —we are civil to each other at dinner, but it's tense.

Rosalie is quiet as we eat.

I look over at her and realize she is crying. Big tears dripping onto her plate. She doesn't bother wiping them.

"What is it, honey?" I say.

"I don't have any friends and I'm not going to make any friends sitting at home."

"Julia is a wonderful friend," Nico says.

"But she is always at her dad's house. Tomorrow is her birthday and she's there. I wanted to give her a present, but I can't even do that."

"I have an idea," I say. "Why don't we send something for her to her dad's house. Maybe one of those really cool flower vases of candy. Have you seen those?"

Rosalie looks up. "Yes."

"Text her and ask for her dad's address. I'll order it right now. We can decide what you want to put on the card, what you want to say."

Rosalie brightens up. Within thirty minutes we've arranged for the gift to arrive with a card from Rosalie.

Dante comes rushing in.

He's smiling.

"He had a good day. He still is struggling to find the right words, but he's doing really good. And he passed a bunch of tests and is using a walker. Although he hates it."

"That's great news!" Nico says. And the way he says it—with such sheer joy and enthusiasm—makes me love him more than ever. But I'm still angry.

But I smile at Dante. "What do you mean he hates it?"

Dante bursts out laughing. "I was there when they brought the walker into his room and told him they wanted him to practice walking with it. At first, he refused and then they told him as soon as he graduated from the walker, he would use a cane. He looked at them and said, 'You've got to be kidding?'"

With Dante there, the tension in the air eases and we break open a bottle of wine.

Rosalie seems happy, too. She's drawing in her sketch pad and then shyly showing us her work. She's drawn me and Nico with our arms around each other.

I smile at Nico. He smiles back. She's a smart kid.

About nine I tell Rosie she should go to bed.

"Why?" she says. "I don't have school anymore."

Dante raises an eyebrow. I shake my head. "That's not true. We're just still figuring out where you are going to go to school. You still should be practicing your math problems and reading."

"I don't consider reading school work," she says indignantly.

I hide my smile.

"Do you want me or your dad to tuck you in?"

"I told you," she says standing. "I'm too old to be tucked in."

"Well goodnight sweetie," I say.

After she kisses and hugs each one of us, she leaves with Django trailing behind.

Dante stretches.

"So."

"Yes?" I say, suddenly on alert at his tone.

"Today Wayne remembered some things."

I lean forward. "Oh, my God. What?"

Dante looks back at the house to make sure Rosie is gone before he speaks.

Apparently, Wayne met with the handyman fixing his boat and they made arrangements for the man to come back the next week.

"He did meet with the handyman?" I ask. "Who is this guy? What's his name?"

Dante smiles. "Already on that. He's worked with the guy for years. Good guy he would trust no matter what. And even if he didn't, guy has an alibi. He had to leave their meeting to go pick his wife up at the airport. The couple then went to their daughter's house in Mission Viejo for dinner and ended up drinking so much they stayed the night. Commander Reeves told Wayne they double checked and could verify it happened."

"Commander Reeves is on this? You talked to her?"

"No, but she's in daily contact with Wayne."

"Good," Nico says.

"After the handyman left, Wayne says he remembers taking a shower and dressing in his favorite Louis Vuitton sweater."

"I love that he remembers exactly what he was wearing," I say wryly.

"You don't even want to know how he reacted when he learned the paramedics had cut the sweater off of him."

I shake my head. But I can't help but laugh.

Just then we hear loud music and laughter from Gloria's backyard.

Dante raises an eyebrow.

"She got a boy," I say.

He nods and continues.

"He asked what happened to his clothes. I found the bag in one of the cupboards in his room. He held the bag upside down and pieces of fabric fell to the ground. It was shredded. I thought he was going to cry."

"God, I love Wayne," I say, laughing.

"He said after he showered and dressed, he headed up to the picnic area to meet Shelby for the barbecue. He says about six people were there, including that Bryce guy, who by the way, is a black belt—"

"Really?" I say.

"And that other dude, Michael, was there, too."

He started to fix himself a burger when Bryce asked him what he wanted to drink, Dante says. After Wayne said he didn't drink, Bryce acted a little bit like a dick, but then came back with an energy drink saying "this is the only thing we have that's nonalcoholic."

Wayne says he took a drink of it.

"And that's the last thing he remembers."

"You're fucking kidding me," I say.

Dante shakes his head. "And get this, the drink was open when Bryce handed it to him."

"Fuck!" I say and stand. "They drugged him and beat him up."

Dante nodded. "That's what I think, too. But why?"

"I think we should go down to the marina and find out," I say.

19

I DRIVE THE LINCOLN DOWN TO THE MARINA.

"What's up with you and Nico?" Dante asks.

"He doesn't think Rosalie should learn to shoot a gun."

"I agree."

"Fuck you," I say.

He laughs.

"Do you really think she needs to learn that?"

"She's been freaked out for a long time," I say. "It got even worse after Wayne was attacked. Nightmares and so on."

"Oh," Dante says.

I glance over at him. "What?"

He shrugs. "I guess I don't know if she should or not, then."

"I think Nico feels the same way. He wants her to have a normal childhood."

Dante snorts. "The former head of one of the world's largest cartel is asking a lot."

"No shit."

I park about a block away from the marina in the Gas Lamp quarter.

"Just so you know," I say as we start to walk. "I've been

banned from the marina. Like if I show my face again I'll be arrested for trespassing."

"Of course you will."

We stop talking about a block from the gate to the marina. The sun has set and it's already pitch black. There is no moon tonight.

Dante looks over at the picnic area and then looks quickly away.

The key card still opens the gate. So that's a good sign. I open it slowly but it still squeaks a little. I close it as quietly as I can and then nod toward the dock.

We make our way under the dim lights. The dock moves and creaks underneath our feet. As soon as we are at Wayne's boat, I crane my neck to see the slip beside his.

Shelby's boat is dark. It seems awfully early for her to have turned in. She must not be there.

Dante whispers to me. "I'm going to go grab some things out of Wayne's boat. I have the key. I left some things there and he wanted me to grab his journal."

"Okay," I say. "I'll wait here."

But I'm lying.

As soon as he steps onboard the back of Wayne's boat, I'm hopping onto Shelby's. The boat rocks under me as I jump onboard.

I freeze until the boat settles down and nobody comes screaming out of the cabin attacking me. I make my way toward the cabin door and try the handle. Fuck. It's locked. I look around the outside part of the boat. Looking for something, although I'm not sure what.

Then I hear voices and panic. Fuck. I leap out of the boat and am casually walking toward his boat when I run into Shelby. She freezes. Her eyes immediately dart to her boat behind me, which fuck it all, is still moving from my jump. She narrows her eyes.

"Hey," I say.

"You're not supposed to be here."

"Yeah. I know. I'm just leaving." I brush by her.

"Not fast enough," she says.

I pause with my back turned to her.

"I can stay longer," I say. Then I turn to face her. "Because I think we have a lot to talk about."

"Fuck you."

I eye her. I'm weighing the wisdom of fucking taking her head off with my hand, and decide it's not the right move. At least not right this second.

"Listen, bitch," I say leaning toward her. She shrinks back so I take a step forward until our faces are inches apart. "I know you know what happened to Wayne. And I'm not going to rest until I find out, too. And I promise if you had anything to do with it, you will pay. And you will pay dearly."

She scowls. "I didn't touch your faggy friend."

She's on the ground before the words are completely out of her mouth. And then she starts to scream. Her nose is bloody. She's holding it screaming and kicking at me. I'm already backed off. Then Bryce comes in and I turn and drop kick him in the balls.

But motherfucker, he is a black belt. And he came back at me with a white-hot fury.

It's been a hell of a long time since I've been in the Dojo. I'd gotten lazy in San Diego. And soft. He outweighs me and is much stronger. It doesn't take much for him to grab me and pin me. My only recourse is to rear back and slam my head into his nose. But he barely flinches. Instead he backhands the side of my head and I see sparks.

"This what you did to Wayne?" I choke the words out. My

hearing is fucked so it sounds like gobbledy gook to my own ears.

Then I get my wits about me enough to lift my foot and slam my boot down on his shin. He yelps, but doesn't loosen his grip. He picks me up and slams me to the dock. Then he's sitting on me with his hands around my neck. He's going to kill me. My vision starts to dim.

"Crazy bitch. Stay out of this."

Then I hear shouting and feel the dock wobbling underneath me from people running.

Someone is shouting that the cops are here.

Bryce is suddenly gone.

Off of me and gone. Then I hear Shelby's boat start up. By the time I crawl to my knees, the boat is heading toward the harbor. I pull myself to a stand and hobble toward Dante who is at the gate holding it open. I'd call it running but it's not even that. I race up the steps and through the gate and smack into a cop.

"Whoa," he says.

I back up. There are two of them. One older with longer dark hair. One younger with a crewcut. Both buff, chests puffed out.

Dante gives me an apologetic look. "I had to call 911."

"We got a call about trespassers."

Dante scowls. "Trespassers? I called 911 because my friend here was being attacked."

The two cops look at one another.

"Yeah, you don't look so hot," the younger cop says. "Who did this to you?"

"They just left in that boat," I say pointing toward the speck that is Shelby's boat leaving the harbor. "As soon as you arrived, they bailed."

"Could we please see some identification?" the older cop asks.

We hand him our licenses. Then one of them talks into the radio for a few seconds away from us and comes back.

"You need an ambulance?"

I make a face.

"She's fine," Dante says and puts his arm around me. "I'll make sure she visits her primary doctor tomorrow."

WE'VE TURNED onto my street when my cell rings.

"I really wish you hadn't gone back to the marina."

It's Commander Reeves.

"Who said I did?"

She doesn't answer.

I pull into my garage and hit the garage door so it closes smoothly behind us.

"I'm home. Where did you think I was?"

She sighs loudly. "You're playing with fire."

"I always do."

"If I have to arrest you for trespassing that's not going to be fun for either one of us."

"Then don't arrest me."

"Listen, I'm not a fan of the crowd at the marina either. And I am definitely keeping tabs on them. All of them."

"Good," I say.

"But they don't know this."

She lets that sink in.

"They have no clue they are suspects?"

"Only clue they have is you showing up fishing for information."

"Point taken," I say. "But you have to understand something. You are, let's say, limited in your investigative methods under the law, correct?"

"I don't think I should hear this," she says.

"Actually, you're right. Bye. Have a good night."

I hang up and grin at Dante.

He rolls his eyes.

When we get home I crawl into bed and snuggle up to Nico.

He wraps me in his arms and hugs me tight.

"How did it go?"

"Frustrating!" I say and sit up. "I know Shelby knows what happened and she refuses to say anything. I mean, hell, maybe she attacked Wayne herself."

"Maybe," Nico says.

We sit in the dark for a few seconds and then Nico starts to kiss my neck. I lean back and soon I forget I was ever angry with him.

And he definitely forgets it, as well.

In the morning, we come out of the bedroom holding hands.

Rosalie, who is sitting at the bar eating cereal, smiles.

"So, does this mean you're taking me to the range, Gia?"

I start laughing. "It means nothing. It means your dad and I still have to talk about it."

Nico nods. "We have not decided."

I love the "we" and so I simply nod in agreement.

Rosalie scoffs and gets up from the table.

I start poking through cupboards and the refrigerator, assessing the food situation.

"I already made a list last night while you were gone," Nico says, reading my mind.

"Of course you did."

I take the piece of paper he offers me and scan it.

"Looks pretty thorough," I say. "I'll shower and go get us some food."

Our informal arrangement is that I shop for food and he cooks. I hate cooking. He hates shopping. I know I definitely get the better end of the deal.

After showering I put on a loose-fitting black maxi dress, my biggest black sunglasses, and some flip flops with red jewels on the straps.

"I miss Julia," Rosalie says as soon as I walk into the room.

"Invite her over," I say. "I'll be back in an hour. Maybe I can take you guys to the beach or something."

"Okay," Rosie says and runs to her room.

Nico is in his office. His busiest time for day trading is early morning since the markets open on Eastern time.

I kiss him on the neck. He's on a call so I don't speak. I lean down and write a note. "Going to get food."

He smiles and nods.

I hate grocery shopping. I hate cooking more. But still.

As I pull out of our driveway I see a car that just pulled out of Gloria's driveway head in the opposite direction. It's a blue truck. Not her gold Cadillac I've seen her driving.

Something about the back of the man's head looks familiar for some reason.

Must be Gloria's boyfriend.

Good for her.

I harbor no ill will toward anyone today.

I'm too damn happy and grateful to be alive.

The day is the kind of brilliant sunny, warm San Diego day that makes the rest of the world hate this city.

I roll down all the windows on the Lincoln and blast my kick-ass sound system, singing along to Victoria Monét's song, *Moment.* I especially love the part where she sings, "This is your motherfuckin' moment," so I sing that especially loud. It may or may not raise some eyebrows as I drive by joggers.

I'm feeling on top of the world.

Wayne is getting better every day. Dante is head over heels in love with him. I love, love, love Nico and am not afraid to shout it from the rooftops. I love Rosalie like she is my own flesh and blood. I feel so blessed to be living this life, to have this little family in San Diego. It's more than I ever hoped or dreamed for.

Tears prick my eyes as I suddenly wish with all my heart that my mother and father were still alive. They would have made wonderful grandparents. And they would have been so happy to see the life I have now.

This is possibly the first time since they were murdered that I think that they might be proud of me if they could see me right now...

20

As I'm driving and thinking about Wayne, I decide I'll go to the marina first. I'll see if Shelby is there and if I can talk her into telling me what happened to Wayne.

Even though my instinct is to kick her ass, today I'm feeling generous and so I'll probably try sweet talking it out of her. I laugh even thinking this.

At the marina, I am nearly at Shelby's boat when that fathead marina manager spots me. He was doing something at someone else's boat and starts to run toward me. He's holding a cell phone. And speaking into it. Fuck.

Then he stands blocking my way back to the stairs leading out of the marina.

I'm considering ploughing through him when I see several police officers coming down the stairs behind him. Motherfucker. They must've been in the neighborhood.

I turn. Shelby has just come onto the deck of her boat. She lights a cigarette and blows the smoke over my head. She is smirking.

"Hope you like jail, bitch," she says. "I'm sure Big Martha is going to like your perky titties and big ass a lot."

I keep my face deadpan. No use giving her any satisfaction.

No use running now. I don't want an evading arrest charge to go along with my trespassing.

He stands there, blocking my way until the cops are beside him. Then he steps aside to let them pass. I stand there watching.

Shelby is snickering behind me.

"I'm not done with you yet," I say to her without turning my head. "Not by a long shot."

Then there is a cop in front of me.

"You just don't learn, do you?" he says and sighs. Shit. Reeves must have told him about me. Or the manager.

"What's to learn? That I have to investigate an assault in San Diego on my own because you bozos have your heads up your ass?"

I feel a little guilty saying it, because Commander Reeves is actually a good one, but the truth is that this should've been solved a long time ago. Wayne nearly died.

"Turn around," the cop says. I do. He snaps cuffs on me. Now, I'm facing Shelby's boat. Before I'm jerked back around, someone comes up onto the deck from below.

I can only see the back of the man's head before the cop yanks me and steers me toward the parking lot. But I know what I saw. A man's head. The same back of the head I saw driving away from Gloria's house today. Bryce.

Holy fucking shit.

He was at Gloria's house.

I start to kick and scream as the cop pushes me forward. "Stop. Let go of me."

Then I'm on my face on the deck and the cop's knees are digging into my back. He leans down by my ear and growls. "Listen bitch. You want to fight? Fight. See what happens. I'll charge you with resisting arrest next. Is that what you want?"

I go limp and say in a meek voice. "No."

I need to let him think I've given in. Because I need to get away from him before he puts me in the cop car. He hauls me to my feet and I cringe as the handcuffs dig into my wrists. Then he kicks me in the back or at least it feels like a kick and takes my breath away.

I keep quiet. As he leads me to the steps leading out of the marina I look around frantically for some way to escape. And then I realize I'm fooling myself. I'm not going anywhere except the jail.

I'm fucked. Totally fucked. A crowd is standing in a semi-circle around us. Even if I got away they would probably tackle me. One big dude looks at me and then spits on the ground. Fucker.

The cops stuff me in the back of the squad car. I want to punch and kick and scream but instead I sit there fuming with rage.

And then as we drive away, I see it. The same car that was leaving Gloria's house. Proof positive that it was Bryce. What the fuck?

I get booked and poked and prodded and thrown in a holding cell. I scream that I want my one phone call and someone just laughs. There is a small rectangular window in the door and I press my face against it and yell again. "I want my phone call."

"You get a call. Just not right away," a voice says on the other side of the door.

"Fuck you!!!!!" I scream with rage.

I'm screaming at my unseen tormenter who is laughing and talking shit just out of my eyesight.

Another inmate across the hall comes to the window and glares at me.

It's a dude with dreadlocks. He sticks out his tongue at me and makes an obscene gesture. I give him the finger. He laughs.

I slump to the ground.

I feel so helpless.

Then I stand up again.

"Get me Commander Reeves."

There is only silence.

I try again. "If she finds out how you're treating me, she's going to ... she's going to ..." I'm not sure what she will do so I finally come up with "She's going to kick your ass."

I press my face to the glass and I see two men talking and looking my way.

Good. Maybe bringing up the commander's name means something.

I soon find out it does.

Within thirty minutes my door opens.

"This way."

I glare but follow the cop.

He leads me down the hall and into a tiny room with a desk and two chairs, one on each side.

Reeves is sitting in one of the chairs. She stands when I come in. "I told you not to go back there."

"I think I know who attacked Wayne," I blurt the words out.

She frowns. "Explain."

So, I do. I tell her everything.

When I'm done, she nods.

"I'll send one of my investigators down to the marina to talk to him."

"Now?"

She sighs. "Yes."

"Can't you go yourself?" I ask, knowing I'm pushing it, but I also add. "My car is still there."

She stares at me for a long moment.

"Let's go," she finally says.

"Really?"

"Hurry, before I change my mind."

I flip off the cop who arrested me as I walk out, trailing behind the commander.

He does a double take.

Reeves doesn't put on lights and sirens on her black Crown Victoria, but we do haul ass. And I appreciate her urgency. I call Nico as we drive.

"I got arrested. I'm out now. I'm with the commander. We're heading to the marina. Bryce, that guy from the marina, was at Gloria's house today. Something is fishy, Nico. Will you head over there to the house and see if Bryce is there? If he went back? And maybe ask Gloria what the fuck? If you can, search the house. She's fucking weird about people in her hall. She's hiding something. And be careful." I blurt it all out in a rush.

Nico says, "I can do it but right now I have a meeting online with some investors on the east coast. I can do it after?"

Reeves hits her steering wheel, startling me. "That was a bad idea. All of it. You might have sent him into a dangerous situation."

I text him. "Never mind. We can bring her cookies or something later when I get home."

He replies. "Got it."

I look at her. "There. You happy? He'll wait until I go with him."

"Like that's any better?" she says.

We are nearly to the marina. But something is bothering me.

Why would Bryce try to kill Wayne?

It doesn't make sense.

When we pull into the parking lot at the marina I can see that Shelby's boat is in its slip. I let us in with the key card. Reeves gives me the side-eye.

"What?"

She doesn't answer and we both are fast walking down the dock and at Shelby's boat. She's in a bikini, oiled up and lying on the front of the boat with a beer.

She lazily sits up.

"I thought you were in jail getting fucked by Big Martha," she says coolly.

I expected her to be more rattled.

The commander takes out her badge.

"I'm looking for a friend of yours. Bryce Gordon. I believe he was here earlier."

I look over in surprise. I didn't know she knew his last name. The commander is more on top of this than I realized.

Shelby shrugs. "I don't know where he is. He comes and goes."

"I'd like to take a look onboard just to make sure he didn't slip under the deck while you were sunbathing."

"You got a warrant?" Shelby sits up and lifts her sunglasses. Her eyes narrow.

"Only the one for your arrest for unpaid traffic tickets. You want that one?" Reeves asks.

I sit back in admiration and watch the woman work.

"Fine," Shelby says standing up. "Come on. I'll show you. Bryce isn't here."

"I think I'd rather look for myself," she says and steps onboard the back end. "You wait here and keep Gia company."

She starts to protest but then closes her mouth.

I give her an evil grin. She opens her mouth in surprise.

"Hope your drug stash is well hidden," I say.

"She can't do shit without a warrant. None of that will hold up in court."

"She doesn't need a warrant. She has probable cause."

"Like what?" she says making a face.

"Like your fucking bong sitting right there," I say.

She looks down.

"Fuck you," she says.

"You know what happened to Wayne," I say and fold my arms across my chest. "That's going to make you an accessory to murder you know."

It works. She looks chocked. "He died?"

"You know the prison time for accessory, right?"

"I'm not an accessory if I just don't snitch to the cops. That doesn't make me an accessory."

"Sure, it does." I say. Inside I'm thrilled. She just admitted she knows.

"It was Bryce, wasn't it? We already know he drugged Wayne. But why? Why would he drug him and hit him?"

She looks away.

"Why are you protecting him anyway?"

She scowls.

"It was an accident anyway." She says this in a low voice. "It would be manslaughter. Not murder."

"Bullshit," I say. "You drugged Wayne. And Bryce hit him. But why?"

She swallows. "I didn't drug anyone."

"But you knew he was drugged. And you know Bryce hit him," I soften my voice. "If you testify, they'll give you immunity."

She looks away again. "Why?"

Shelby squirms uncomfortably.

"Are you afraid?" I say. "Are you afraid something bad will happen to you if you talk? I mean other than your dickhead manager evicting you because he doesn't want bad publicity?"

She looks like she is about to say something. I am holding my breath. But the moment is lost because the boat shifts and she turns away from me.

Reeves comes back up and steps onto the deck. Without a word, she turns and leaves heading back toward the parking lot. I follow.

"Shelby basically admitted that she knew Wayne had been drugged and hit," I say.

"Our investigators are having a hard time getting witnesses to come forward," the commander says. "And we're not sure why."

"Why would someone do that to Wayne? I mean now that we know he was drugged and it wasn't just someone who got mad and hit him."

She stands by her car and turns to me. "It's really going to be up to what Wayne remembers to figure out motive. Although you and Dante can possibly still help with figuring out why someone would want to drug and attack him."

"It doesn't make any sense," I say as she unlocks her door.

"Most criminals don't," she says.

I'm so lost in thought I don't realize I've spoken out loud until the Commander stops opening her car door and turns toward me.

"What?" I say.

"What did you just say?"

"I said it would make sense if someone attacked me or," I almost say Nico, but remember his witness protection name of Damien. "Or Damien. But attacking Wayne makes no sense."

Her eyes bore into me. "Why would it make sense if someone attacked you or Damien, Gia? What aren't you telling me?"

Fuck. Fuck. Fuck.

I am staring at her and finally I say. "A lot. I'm not telling you a lot."

"God, DAMN it!" she says.

"It's not pretty," I say.

"Gia? We may have devoted all of our resources in the wrong direction because you haven't been forthright with us —with me."

I turn to her angrily. "Why would I ever suspect that someone would go after Wayne—my best friend's new boyfriend—to get to me? It doesn't make any sense."

"That's a question for you to answer."

I text Dante, who is at the hospital.

"Does Wayne remember anything else? I'm with the commander right now."

"No. But he took pictures at the barbecue. It shows that Bryce guy. You want it for the cops? We were going to show her next time she came by."

"Yeah. Send it now."

I turn to the commander. "We got a picture of Bryce. Wayne took it the night of the barbecue."

My phone buzzes. The photo comes through. Before I really look at it, I forward it to Reeves and then we both look at our phones and blow the picture up.

It's a picture of about six people gathered around a picnic table and grill. It also shows the edge of the parking lot. I study the faces. Shelby. Bryce. Michael. And three people I don't recognize.

The commander points to them. "We can't find those three. We were told they were down from L.A. and are back home. Your friend Shelby is being less than helpful. Says she only knew their first names."

"Shelby is a lying bitch," I say.

The commander's face remains expressionless. I suppose she has to be professional.

But she didn't argue with me, did she?

"See you around," I say and walk away.

As I pull away I see that she's still sitting in her car.

21

I'M UNLOADING WHAT FEELS LIKE THE MILLIONTH BAG OF
groceries from the Lincoln onto the kitchen counter feeling so
much loathing for this asinine task.

From now on I'm shopping online and either picking up the
order or having it delivered.

Shopping is ridiculous.

It takes so much time.

I told Rosalie I'd be no more than an hour and it's five hours
later. Django whines at me.

"I know," I tell him. "I'm a sucky mom today."

Or mom figure. Most moms don't leave for the grocery store
and end up in jail. Whatever.

Finally, I haul in the last bag of groceries and then steel
myself to unload it all and put it away. Django follows me into
the garage and back to the kitchen for every trip, whining.

"What?" But I'm busy so I ignore him.

When I've put away every last item and stacked the last
canvas grocery bag, Nico walks in.

"Good timing, sailor," I say and roll my eyes.

He laughs. "All you had to do was ask. I would have been happy to come in and help you."

"Sure." I say in a tone of disbelief but I'm smiling.

"Ready to go bring Stripper Mom some cookies and see if that dickwad is there hiding?"

"Stripper Mom?" He takes me in his arms and kisses my brow.

I pull back. "Here," I toss him a bag of coffee beans. "You can put that away. One of the one million items I just had to put away."

"One million?"

"At least."

"Gia, just call me into the kitchen next time, I'd be happy to help you. Besides, why didn't Rosalie help?"

"Like you, she hid when I got home," I say.

He draws back so sharply, I jump.

"What?"

He has a terrible look on his face.

"She's not with you?" His words are calm, deadly and measured.

I feel terror swarm over me.

I don't answer. Instead, I push past him and start yelling, "Rosie?" and race to her room. It's empty. I look in the living room. Empty. I check the patio. Empty. We race around screaming her name until we are face-to-face in the kitchen again. Django races after us.

"Oh, my God," I say.

"When did you last see her?" he asks.

"Right before I left," I say frantically. "I told her I'd be back in an hour and that I would take her and Julia to the beach."

He frowns.

"What the fuck, Nico? I told you I was arrested and taken to jail. What did you think that she was in the jail cell with me?"

He shakes his head. "I've been so caught up in work today. I didn't think."

"When did you last see her?"

"I saw her earlier. When she was eating cereal," he says.

I dial her cell number. It goes straight to voice mail. But then I hear some buzzing. I follow the noise. Rosie's phone is on the ground by the front door. We never go in or out the front door. Or at least very rarely. We usually go in through the garage. I pick up her phone. There is a litany of missed messages and notifications from friends.

It is fucking ominous that Rosie is somewhere without her phone. Dread floods through me. That kid, like others, is attached to her phone. Something is wrong. Very fucking wrong.

I'm already out the door and running down our sidewalk to the road.

He's on my heels. The only thing I can think of is that she went to Julia's house. It still doesn't explain why she would go without her phone. But I have to check Julia's house. Where that fuckwad Bryce might be.

Nico and I arrive breathless at Gloria and Julia's front door. I'm pounding the door and punching the doorbell.

"She has to be here," I say. "She has to."

Nico doesn't answer.

After what feels like an eternity, Gloria opens the door with a smile.

"Hi, you two."

I want to punch her but instead I say, "Is Rosalie here?" I look past her for a sign of Rosalie. Or Bryce.

Her face crinkles. "No?" she says it as a question.

"Are you sure?" I ask. "Is there any chance she came over to see Julia without you knowing and the two are playing in Julia's room?"

My voice is shrill. Everything feels surreal and my stomach is clenched.

Now her eyes grow wide. "No. This is Julia's weekend at her father's house."

I nearly collapse.

Nico grabs me.

"Can we come in?" he asks.

She hesitates and for a second I wonder if she has a visitor. Her boyfriend.

It would explain the low-cut dress that is so short it probably barely covers her underwear. If she's even wearing any.

She holds the door and Nico heads straight to the kitchen faucet. He opens a cupboard and takes out a glass that he fills with water from the tap. For a second my eyes narrow. How did he know which cupboard held the glasses? But any suspicion fades when I see how he ignores Gloria completely to focus on me.

He hands me the water. He looks so concerned. "Are you okay, Gia?"

I shake my head. "No. Not until we find Rosalie."

He nods. "She has to be somewhere close. Let's go drive around the neighborhood and look for her."

He is focusing on me. Behind him I see Gloria shoot a strange glance down the hall. The hall with all the locked doors. Is there a man here in her bedroom or something?

"Excuse me," she says. "I was just about to leave."

Nico gives her a tight smile. "Sorry. We'll leave now. Please let me know if you hear from Rosalie by chance."

She walks us to the door. We are in our own driveway when I think of something. "Go get the car," I say to Nico. "I just thought of something."

Gloria opens the door before I can knock. Again, I look past her for some sign of Rosalie or Bryce.

"Can I have Julia's phone number?" I say. "I want to see if she's heard from Rosalie. Rosie's not picking up her phone."

I don't tell her that I have Rosie's phone in my pocket. It's an excuse to see how she reacts when I come back. To see if there was someone else in the house.

Something flashes across Gloria's face. Something I don't like but don't have time to worry about. She reels off the number and closes the door on me.

Nico is starting to pull down the driveway so I run and get in the passenger door.

I lean over my phone and dial Julia's number, but there is no answer. I leave a short message. "This is Gia. Is Rosalie with you? If not, did she call you today? Please call me back at this number."

I realize I should've asked Gloria for Julia's dad's number.

Meanwhile, we are driving up and down the streets of our neighborhood. We stop and ask people if they have seen a little girl with long dark hair. Nobody has.

Finally, I call Commander Reeves.

I'm beside myself with worry.

"I know you don't handle stuff like this, but our daughter is missing. This has never happened before."

She hesitates but then says normally she would transfer me to someone else, but that she will handle it for me.

Then we hang up.

I dial Julia's number again. No answer.

Nico is pulled over to the side of the road with his head on the steering wheel.

"It's too early to panic," he says, almost as if he's speaking to himself.

Then I think of something. "What if she came home while we were out?"

Back home we search the house, again calling her name. Nothing.

I slump in the corner of the kitchen floor and put my head in my hands.

"Think, Gia," I say partly to myself. "Think. Where could she be?"

"She did not just wander off," Nico says. He is pacing the kitchen.

His words make my stomach turn.

I stand up. "You really think someone took her?"

He nods, running his hands through his hair. The look he gives me is deadly. As if he could kill me with his bare hands. But I know it's not meant for me.

"Who? And why?"

We stare at one another. Both of us have more enemies than fingers and toes. Damn it all.

"Do you think it's related to Wayne's attack?" I finally say.

Nico looks at me and nods. "I think it might be."

I open my phone and scan the picture of the crowd at the barbecue. The three people from L.A. don't look suspicious. Two women and a guy with his arm around one of the women. But then again, your next-door neighbor serial killer never stands out, either.

I set the phone down. But then immediately pick it back up.

Something was there that I was looking at and didn't realize was important. At first.

The edge of the photo showed the marina parking lot and a few cars. One of the cars is a gold Cadillac.

I take off running out the door with my phone.

Nico is right behind me.

I'm pounding on the door of Gloria's house. She's not answering.

Her garage door doesn't have windows.

I keep pounding and ringing the doorbell. Her door is solid. Maybe even steel.

I'm shouting now. "Gloria! Gloria?"

Nothing.

I go around the side of the house to the wall we share. There is a gate, but it's solid and locked. There is barbed wire at the top. Odd.

Then I have an idea.

"I'm going to need your help," I tell Nico.

As soon as we are back inside our house, I race into the bedroom and get my gun. Nico doesn't say a word, but goes into the gun safe in his closet and takes out a rifle.

In our backyard, Nico sets up a ladder against the wall. There is no barbed wire on the portion of the wall separating our two backyards. I tuck my gun in my waistband and climb the ladder. It's a ten foot drop to the ground below on the other side. I ease myself over quickly, hanging by my hands and easily land on my feet.

Nico follows.

We creep toward the house. The sliding glass door is not locked.

"Gloria?" Nico says as we step inside. "It's Nico. Are you home?"

Nothing. We creep toward the hall.

Slowly we push open doors. First the bathroom. Empty. Then a child's bedroom. Nobody. Then Gloria's large master bedroom. I search the closet and bathroom in there and then we go to the next door.

It's locked.

Nico rears back and kicks it. But nothing happens.

"Is anyone in there?"

My heart is pounding as I put my ear to the door. I don't hear a sound.

I want to just shoot off the lock but don't want to take the chance that Rosalie is somewhere in the room and could be shot.

Nico disappears to look for a tool box in the garage. I hear a door open and close and then he's back with an electric drill. In a few seconds, he's taken the hinges off the door.

When we finally see into the room I rear back in shock at what I see.

22

"HOLY FUCK, NICO."

At first glance, the room appears to be a tidy office. There is a large desk with several monitors and a laptop. It's the pictures on the wall that are fucked up.

They are all of Nico. They are photos of him that I've never seen before. He's always been so careful about having his picture taken. It's one reason we felt so safe in the witness protection program. The wall is also plastered with copies of newspaper articles about him with headlines, such as "Drug Lord Disappears" and "Head of Mexico's Largest Cartel a Mystery Man."

Then, on the opposite wall, there is a shrine.

It's to her son.

There is a table that is covered in dozens of framed photos of the boy. From when he was born to a macabre picture of him in a casket. The table also contains a baseball glove and ball, a chess set, a video game controller, and other memorabilia.

On the wall above is a giant blown up photo of him with Gloria. They are hugging and smiling. The photo is surrounded by a few newspaper articles about the boy and how he overdosed on heroin from Mexico.

Nico and I stand silently and take it all in.

She is after Nico. She's been after Nico for a long time.

The question is did she do all this before Nico moved in next door? Imagine what it was like when she realized that the object of her hatred was her neighbor?

I can't believe that. It is more likely that when she met Nico and figured out who he really was, she directed all her grief about her son's death to Nico and blamed him.

Either way, this meant that there was a good chance she had Rosalie.

I whirl toward Nico. "Was her Cadillac in the garage?"

He shakes his head. "No."

"Where could they be?" They, as in Gloria and Bryce.

I have no idea. I want to cry. Rosalie could be anywhere. Anywhere. I don't know where she is. I don't know if she's dead or alive. I feel so helpless.

Nico snaps his fingers in my face.

"Gia! Gia!"

I shake my head. He puts his hands on my shoulders.

"We will find her."

I don't answer. If I open my mouth I'm going to scream.

I'm going to scream that he doesn't fucking know that. That he doesn't know a goddamn thing.

But I don't say a word.

23

BACK AT THE HOUSE, NICO CALLS 911.

While he's on the phone, I dial Commander Reeves.

"Rosalie, our daughter, is gone," I say. My voice is shaking. I'm on the verge of tears and hysteria. "I think Bryce and our neighbor, Gloria, have her. Her house has a shrine to her dead son. And one wall full of photos of my partner."

I spit it all out in a hurried rush.

"Damien?"

"Yes."

"Why would she have pictures of him, Gia?"

"His name isn't really Damien."

"Who is he?"

I close my eyes and say it, "Nico Ortiz Morales."

"*El Jefe*? The cartel leader?"

I nod, and then realize she can't see me.

"The very one."

"Good God."

"He's in witness protection."

Nico shoots me an alarmed look. He takes his own phone away from his ear and looks at me in surprise.

"What's your address?" Reeves asks.

I reel it off. "Her house is the yellow one just north of ours."

"I'm sending a squad right now. Don't move."

I hang up and grab my keys—and his—off the hook by the door.

Nico shouts after me but I'm gone. I'm backing out of the garage by the time he races in there. He is shouting and starts to chase after me, but I squeal out of the driveway and down the road.

I know I'm desperate but I just have this feeling that one person knows where Rosie is and I'm going to make her tell me.

I need to do this on my own.

Because someone is going to die or get arrested for murder.

And I can't guarantee it won't be me.

Nico has to stay safe at home.

Because if Rosalie is alive and I find her, she's going to need a parent.

24

Down at the marina, I don't even try to be quiet as I race down the wobbly dock to Shelby's boat. It's already dark. She's not topside but there is a light on below. I jump onto the backside of her boat and then shove open the door. She is sitting there filing her nails and watching TV. She screams when she sees me. But I'm already on her.

I stick the gun under her chin.

"No more fucking games. As soon as you involved my daughter, you signed your death warrant, bitch. Where is she?"

Shelby starts crying. "I swear I didn't know they were going to take the girl. I told them it was a bad idea."

"Fuck you. Where is she?" I press the gun harder into her chin.

"Gloria said she'll kill me if I talk."

"I'll kill you if you don't." Hearing Gloria's name enrages me.

"Gloria said it would just be Wayne. That she wanted Bryce to hit him as a warning to you guys."

"Where the fuck is Rosalie?"

"Bryce has her. He's meeting Gloria out by the old shipwreck. They left a little while ago."

"The SS Monte Carlo."

She reaches for a pen and paper.

"Don't fucking move."

"I have to give you the compass coordinates. That's the best way to find it at night."

I let her write. She keeps talking.

"Gloria is using Bryce. He's in love with her. He'll do anything she says. She showed up here like she hung out at the bar all the time, but now I know she was just pretending to get to Wayne. And your daughter."

I nod. "She's using you, too, Shelby."

She swallows. "I know."

"And a little girl might die because of it."

"I know," she says in a choked voice.

I take the gun away from her chin.

"Where are the keys to your boat?"

"What?" she blinks.

I shove the gun up to her eyeball. "Your keys?"

She points to a small ceramic bowl on the table. I pluck the keys out.

"Now you're going to slowly walk up topside and show me how to start your boat and steer it and where your compass is."

She doesn't answer.

"Do you fucking understand?"

"I..." she starts to say.

I push the gun further in her eye socket. "The only reason I'm not making you drive us is out of mercy. Because if you did drive, there's a good chance you might end up dead. So, are you going to cooperate and show me and then get off your damn boat or not?"

She nods.

A few seconds later, I'm navigating out of the marina into the harbor, heading for the shipwreck and Rosalie.

25

THE WIND WHIPS MY HAIR IN FRONT OF MY EYES BLOCKING MY view.

I glance down at the compass. I'm close. Very close.

But then I see the boat. Or at least what I think is the boat.

It's a long less dark silhouette on the dark sea.

Thank God. I'm almost there.

Before I can react, the entire sky lights up in an orange glow at the same time I both hear and feel the blast of an explosion rolling across the water toward me.

I'm too late. She's dead.

I'm screaming and momentarily blinded, but I don't stop the boat.

I keep steering it right into the inferno, scanning the water around the flaming boat for any sign of life.

No. No. No. I've stopped screaming out loud, but I'm chanting this in my head.

I see debris floating around the burning boat that is sinking under the waves.

Nothing that was on the boat could have survived the blast.

The realization makes me weak in the knees. I clutch the steering wheel so I don't collapse in a heap.

And still I refuse to admit it.

"Rosie!" I scream as I grow closer, but my boat's engine drowns out my voice.

"Rosie!" Then I'm there and I cut the engine, letting the boat drift, crawling up on the front deck searching the dark waters. My eyes scan the burning surface of the sinking boat. I search the dark floating hunks of debris. And then I think I see something. Something clinging to a floating piece of the boat

It's Rosalie.

26

Huddled in the boat, Rosalie is shivering. I worry she's going into shock.

When I was idling over to her to fish her out of the water, I heard another boat approach.

Gloria.

Then I heard the boat turn around and take off.

My first instinct was to take off after her.

But I needed to get Rosalie.

Gloria would escape. For now.

Then I had Rosalie in my arms and was holding her vowing to never let her go again.

I took her under the deck and bundled her up in every piece of bedding there is. Then I turned on the heater full blast and hugged her.

"Are you okay?" I ask her now. Her teeth are chattering.

"He's dead."

She must be talking about Bryce.

"I know."

"I killed him."

"What?" I try to keep my voice neutral.

"I made the boat explode."

"You did?"

"Yes. When I heard your boat coming I did it. And then I jumped overboard."

"How did you do it?"

"I used my knife to cut the fuel line while he was on the radio in the cabin. Then I found a lighter."

We've been treating her like a baby. We've underestimated her. She may be 11 in years, but she's fifty in life experiences.

"What knife?" I say it lightly.

She looks down. "I took a knife from dad's dresser."

"How long have you had it?"

"Since Wayne."

"Okay," I say.

"He was going to kill you. He said so. Then he was going to kill me. We were just waiting for Julia's mom. Why would Julia's mom want to kill me? I went over there to ask Julia to come over and he was there. And she told me to come inside. Then when he put me in his car, she didn't do anything to stop him, Gia. She let him take me."

Her voice is so full of hurt. It's so forlorn sounding.

I don't answer.

"Gia? Am I evil?"

"Because you killed him?"

She nods.

"No," I say. "But I think we need to talk about that later, okay?"

"Okay," she says.

"You ready to go home?" I ask.

"Yes."

But as soon as I come topside, I see a line of police boats heading our way. I sit back to wait for them. There's going to be some explaining to do.

As the first boat grows closer, I recognize the tall figure standing near the boat operator. My heart floods with love.

Nico.

"Rosie?" I shout. "Your dad is here!"

She races up the stairs. She's not smiling. She's looking around frantically. Then when she sees her dad, her face lights up in joy.

"Daddy!"

As soon as Nico and Rosie reunite, I finally relax. In fact, I'm pretty sure my bones have turned to jelly. I can barely stand.

I huddle in the back of the police boat wrapped in blankets.

A deputy agrees to drive Shelby's boat back to the marina. I'm spent.

All I can do is hug Nico and Rosalie.

As we head back to shore, all I want to do is crawl in a warm bed and sleep for a month. But I know it's probably still hours before we can head home.

I'm right.

They want Rosalie to stay the night at the hospital for observation, but when she reassures them she is fine, the doctor agrees to release her to our care.

"I see no reason to keep her. She's a hardy little soul, isn't she?" she asks.

"That she is," Nico answers.

The police question us and her at the hospital, which saves time.

Reeves makes sure we get it over with as quickly as possible.

I'm so grateful.

She takes me aside before we leave.

"We can't find Gloria."

I nod. I don't tell her that I have a feeling I know where she is. Or where she is heading.

27

THE DRIVE HOME FROM THE HOSPITAL IS A SILENT ONE.

I sit in the back seat holding Rosalie. She is fast asleep.

Every once in a while, I meet Nico's eyes in the rearview mirror. It's too hard to tell what he's thinking from the small slice of his eyes, but I try to smile back at him.

I lean down and kiss the top of Rosalie's head. Precious girl.

When we pull onto our street, I immediately see the cluster of cars in front of Gloria's place. The investigators are scouring her house and gathering evidence.

I see a man come out with a box and load it into the back of a van. I have a feeling they will be there all night. The man briefly looks over at our vehicle and then pauses as if he recognizes Nico. He probably does. If he saw Gloria's wall, he knows who Nico really is.

The man gives us a slight nod. Nico returns it.

I've been a nervous wreck that someone who knows the entire story will rat out Nico. Now, the entire police department knows. We are going to have to move.

It will break my heart, but I will go anywhere to keep my family safe. No question.

Then I think of Rosalie and how she is going to have to make new friends.

I can't imagine her still keeping in touch with Julia. Their friendship is another casualty of all of this. It makes me sad in so many ways. Rosalie needs a friend her own age. But it seems unlikely that this will happen. She is so different than any other child in her grade. She is wise beyond her years. But maybe she can find someone else like Julia—a sweet girl who accepted Rosalie for the person she really was.

My heart goes out to Julia. Thank God, she has been with her father this entire time. But she must be so confused and in so much pain. I hope her father is a good man. Because she will most likely be raised by him from here out. Her new home will be far away from here.

That is, if justice is served.

And I'm hopeful it will be.

With Reeves in charge, leading the investigation on some level, I know there will be no loose ends. It's comforting to have her on our side.

But there is one loose end that I must take care of myself.

Rosalie is still asleep when we pull into our garage. Nico comes around and lifts her from my arms. She wraps her arms around his neck and snuggles into him as he carries her to bed. I follow and watch him tuck her in by the glow of the nightlight.

He pulls the covers up to her chin. She's back asleep.

We stand and watch her, holding hands, for a long time.

Her room, full of pinks and stuffed animals and dolls, is that of a child.

But she is much more than that. She is a warrior. A fighter. A survivor.

As I glance around I see her Karategi, her karate uniform. It's hanging on the wall on a hanger as if it is an art piece. On a small table underneath, she has laid out a book—a book that I never expected to see. It's my own copy of Sun Tzu's, "The Art of War." from our living room bookshelf.

Beside it is a small, flat, oval stone I've never seen before. And beside that is a framed photo. It is of me, Nico, and Rosalie.

Everything is cleared away from this wall. It's starkness only highlights that what remains there is important, sacred, even.

I nudge Nico and jut my chin to the wall with the makeshift shrine.

We have viewed her as a little girl, a child, for far too long.

She is much more than that.

Even with my arguments for the martial arts classes, I still saw her as a little girl. I wanted to believe she could remain innocent.

And she can. In some ways.

Nico looks at the items on the wall and then back at me. He nods.

I don't know what it means.

We head to the bedroom. While he is in the bathroom, I scribble a quick note and leave it on his pillow. "Back soon."

I wait until I'm a few blocks away before I pull over and search my phone.

When we sent Julia her birthday present at her dad's, Rosalie had texted me the address.

Boom.

I set my GPS and go.

If Gloria knows she has to go into hiding, she's damn well either going to grab Julia and take her with her or at the very least say goodbye to her.

That's where I'll find her. I'm certain.

As long as I get there in time.

I do a quick drive by the address. It's a large house in the hills above San Diego. All the lights are off. I don't see a gold Cadillac anywhere.

I have Rosalie's phone so I send a quick text.

"You up?"

"Yea."

"You still at your dad's house?"

"Yes. Why?"

"Your mom didn't come over?"

"???"

"Oh, I was hoping you were coming home today."

"No. Why r u still awake?"

"Long story. Talk to you tomorrow."

Good. She's still there. And her mother hasn't been there yet.

I slump in my seat pulling my baseball cap low. It is quiet. There are no cars coming or going. I've drifted off when I hear the low rumble of an engine beside me. I glance over and jump. It's Gloria in her car staring at me. As soon as she realizes it's me, she floors it and is gone. It takes me a second to start my car and then I'm peeling out after her.

She's taking corners at an insane speed, wobbling on two tires while the other two lift slightly off the ground. I slow because the Lincoln is top heavy and I would easily flip. But on the straight away I gain on her. We race through the dark streets in the hills above San Diego until we are suddenly in rural land. And still she is hauling ass. We have long stretches of straight-away but I can't quite seem to catch up.

I'm swearing and pounding the steering wheel, wishing I was on my old motorcycle or Ferrari instead of my big clunky safe Lincoln. Mom car. I mean the Lincoln can go. But not like my Ferrari did.

Suddenly the Cadillac's tail lights disappear. Fuck. She turned off her lights.

It's only when she speeds past me going the other way that I realize what she's done.

By the time I slow and turn around, I know I've probably lost her. But then a few miles later I come upon a terrible car crash.

The Cadillac is on the side of the road with its front end smashed and a shattered windshield. The front seat is empty and the driver's door is wide open. The other car is a huge truck. The grill is a little pushed in. A guy is standing by it on a cell phone. I skid to a stop.

"Are you okay?"

"I'm fine, my buddy here was bleeding, but we got him patched up."

He gestured toward a guy I didn't notice who is sitting on the curb. His knee is bandaged.

I look over at the Cadillac. The guy sees my gaze.

"That lady was bleeding out of her head. She took off running over there. I was going to try to stop her, but my buddy needed me. I think she's in shock. I'm trying to get through to 911."

I start to race into the brush. I use the flashlight on my phone. She left a trail of blood. I follow the red that is scattered on the desert brush and dirt. I'm nearly out of breath when I come upon her. She is leaning against a tree. She glares at me when I pull up short before her. I take the gun out of my back waistband.

"Tell me why I shouldn't put a bullet in your head right here and now," I say.

I have one hand on my gun and my other hand is shining my phone's flashlight on her.

She smiles. "Because I might die anyway."

"True."

I put my gun away.

"But that's not why. I'm not going to kill you because I want you to suffer in prison for what you did to Wayne and Rosalie."

She spits on the ground. It's blood.

"What about how your husband has made me suffer? My son, my sweet son, got hooked on heroin. He turned into someone I didn't know. He lied. He stole things. And then, you know what? He died. He overdosed."

"I know, Gloria."

"Your husband was the head of a drug cartel," she says and narrows her eyes. "He has blood on his hands."

I swallow. "He's not responsible for your son getting hooked on drugs and overdosing. Have you ever heard of free will?"

"Fuck you!" She screams it. I wince. I hate it, but I wince.

"I get that you wanted to punish him," I say slowly. "What I don't get is why you went after Wayne and Rosalie."

"Wayne just fell into my hands. I followed you guys down to the marina that one day and after you left, I met Bryce. He and I hit it off. And he told me he hated Wayne. I hated Wayne too."

I shake my head. "Why would you hate Wayne?" It makes no sense. Wayne is kind and fun and just a good guy.

"He's a fag."

"You're a loser," I say back.

"Bryce knows. At first, we were just going to give him something to make him stupid. Everybody at the marina likes him so much. We just wanted him to look foolish. And at first, he was. He was stumbling around all stupid. But then Bryce got mad at him and punched him. It was an accident, really. I don't think Bryce wanted him to die. But maybe he did. I don't know."

I am dismayed. It was all an accident. A joke gone wrong? But then they took Rosalie. It doesn't make sense.

"Why would you, a mother, take Rosalie?"

"I recognized Nico at the bus stop a few months ago. And I wanted to kill him. With my bare hands. But then I thought of a better plan. I just didn't know how to do it until I met Bryce," she says. "After Bryce hit Wayne I told him that unless he helped me

I would go to the cops about what he did to Wayne. He was afraid of me."

"I find that hard to believe."

"He was. I had him meet with my lawyer and my lawyer said if anything ever happened to me, the video I took on my phone that night would go to the cops."

"You videotaped Wayne's beating?"

"Yes, I did."

I hear sirens on the distance. I need her to tell me why she took Rosalie.

"Why Rosalie? Why have Bryce take her?"

"I wanted Nico to know what it was like to lose a child," she says and spits the words out. "The only way to punish him was to have him live the rest of his life in the same agony that I am living."

Just then two paramedics race up through the brush.

I step aside. A police officer follows.

Gloria gives me a look.

I turn to the officer. "This woman is wanted for kidnapping," I say. "You can verify it with Commander Reeves of the San Diego Police Department. Her name is Gloria Bleeker."

Then I walk away.

———

WHEN I GET HOME and slip into bed, Nico grabs me and makes love to me fiercely as if it is our last time ever. I rise to his need. The emotions we've experienced the past few days cannot be expressed in any other way right now. This is what we have to share with one another. This is the purest expression of our love for each other.

After ,as I lie there beside him, I realize that we have not spoken since the hospital. And I'm okay with that. What we feel is too much for mere words.

I fall asleep in his arms, my head on his shoulder. I know I will probably get a cramp in my neck from falling asleep like this and I could care less.

I wake later in the night to Nico pacing in the dark in front of our French windows leading to the patio.

"Nico?"

"She needs to learn to fight," he says.

I sit up.

"I want Rosalie to be able to take down a grown man. I want her to know how to kill if it will save her life."

I am out of bed now with my arms wrapped around him from behind.

His entire body is tense. Then it shudders and I realize he is crying.

I hold him tighter.

"I only wanted to give her a normal childhood, Gia," he says.

"I know. But you are giving her a lot more than that, Nico," I say. "You are giving her your love and care. You are the best father a girl could have. And I know because I had an amazing father."

He turns in my arms. His tears are gone.

"She must learn from the best," he says.

I smile in the dark. "I know just the right person."

EPILOGUE

The day of the wedding is gorgeous—warm with clear blue skies.

Then again, every day in San Diego is damn near perfection.

Dante and Wayne are wearing matching Dior suits. Of course. Wayne wears a gray silk tie. Dante's is ecru (I called it beige and was corrected).

The wedding is at the Culver Club in La Jolla.

A while ago, when Wayne said he wanted to marry at the club, I told him I would take care of the arrangements. I was told they had the choice of a ceremony on the actual beach or a cliff-side venue overlooking the water.

Cliffside. Dark memories of Positano flashed before me.

Matt and Dante flushed with love on the Italian cliff proclaiming their commitment to the world. Looking at Bobby and realizing I was ready to marry him.

Hours later, bloodshed at the hotel reception. So many dead and injured. My Bobby. And soon, Matt.

"There's two choices at the club," I said. "One is on the beach. Like in the sand."

"Um, sand would totally ruin my shoes," Dante said. "I don't think I can deal with sand. It's like getting married in the dirt."

"Totally," Wayne agreed.

So, I booked the cliffside. But I didn't call it that. I called it the grassy knoll.

"What's the other venue like?" Wayne asked.

"It, um, has a great view of the ocean," I said.

But Dante knew. He looked at me and I saw his Adam's apple bob as he swallowed. I nodded.

It was cliffside.

But when we arrived, Dante just turned to me and grabbed me in a big hug.

"It's wonderful."

It *is* perfect. A grassy plateau with a flowered arch and behind the couple—the ocean in all its glory.

We only have about 50 people in the white wooden chairs. Small and intimate is what they requested.

The ceremony is brief and a tear jerker.

Soon we are inside the club toasting the couple and dancing and crying and laughing.

Nico takes me in his arms and leads me around the dance floor as Rosalie dances with the two grooms.

"You okay?" Nico asks.

I don't answer at first. I let myself really think about it.

Then I press my face into his shoulder and nod.

"You sure?" he says and draws back.

"Yes, that's why I didn't answer right away. I wanted to think about it."

His face lights up in a smile. "I'm so glad. I knew this day would be hard for you."

I nod. "I still think I'll feel completely relieved once they get in a car and leave the reception."

Nico frowns. "That's a little post-traumatic stress disorder if you ask me."

I give a wry grin. "Yeah. Probably."

We sit back down and I pour another glass of wine. It's more than I usually drink. But I need something to take the edge off.

Rosalie comes over with Eva.

"I think I should take her home to finish packing," my aunt says. "We leave early in the morning."

I shoot a glance at Nico. He sighs. He knows it's best, but it's still going to break our goddamn hearts.

We have decided to send Rosalie to live with Eva for at least a year.

She will train her in her boot camp. Not to become an assassin. Well, yes, to become an assassin, but more so that Rosalie has the skills to defend herself in any situation she could ever find herself in.

Some of Eva's former soldiers have gone on to have highly classified jobs as assassins for world powers. It's not Eva's first choice. But the reputation of Eva's soldiers has grown and it now attracts young women from around the world. They are highly vetted. Eva makes sure they take psych screenings and aren't doing it for the wrong reasons.

Eva herself no longer needs to train women to fight the other mob bosses. She is now the undisputed Queen. Not only is she the Queen of Spades, she is the queen of all the other mob families. She has effectively shut down sex trafficking, which was always her goal.

Nico and I decided to send Rosalie to training as long as we spend part of the time living there, as well. We will go to visit for a month at a time, three times a year. It is the only way to make the time away from her bearable.

Rosalie hugs us both goodnight.

"Will you come tuck me in when you get home?" she asks us.

"Of course," we both say at the same time and laugh.

"Rose, will you go wait by the coat rack?" Eva says. "I want to talk to your dad and Gia privately for a second."

"Sure," she says, but she looks annoyed. At least Eva didn't try to hide the fact that she didn't want Rosalie to hear. I respected that. Rosalie was too smart to hide things from.

We all turn to watch her walk over to where the coats are hung.

"You call her Rose?" I say when Eva turns back.

Eva shrugs. "She requested it."

"Oh," I say.

"I wanted to make sure you were one hundred percent on board with this," Eva says and her face crinkles.

I look at Nico as I nod. "I am."

"Nico?" she says.

"I am. I hate that I am. But I am."

Eva smiles. "She is in good hands."

Nico stands and smiles. "Of that, I have no doubt."

We watch Eva leave. Rosalie's face lights up when my aunt grows closer and I can see her start talking animatedly. I know it's the right thing to do.

This is such a bittersweet moment. Everything is going to change starting in the morning. Rosalie is leaving. But so are we. We're moving at the end of the month. Nico's "handler" in the witness protection program said we fucked up. He's not sure where we will end up. Maybe San Diego. Maybe fucking Idaho. Who knows?

A few hours later, once Dante and Wayne safely get in their livery car and drive off, we head home.

In our own livery car, I lean on Nico and sigh.

"Can you relax now?" he asks.

I shake my head. "No. Now I have to worry about Rosalie."

He laughs. But then he grows serious. "That's how it is to love, Gia."

"I know. Oh, believe me, I know."

Rosalie is asleep when we get home. We both look down on her and smile. I kiss her on the forehead and she murmurs but doesn't wake.

———

In the morning, I'm so nervous, I can barely drink my coffee.

I definitely can't eat. But I try to be chipper.

I know Rosie is in good hands with Eva.

When Nico and I shared custody of Rosalie, I got used to sending her off for a few months, but this feels different. I know when I see her next she is going to be changed.

It scares me. I just hope we are doing the right thing.

We were able to get special passes to walk her to the gate.

I vow not to cry when I say goodbye to her. I manage to hide my tears until she is on board. But I squeeze her long and hard. I bury my face in her hair and try to memorize her smell.

By the time I draw back, I've managed to control my tears. I cried this morning when I woke up but seem to be able to keep my tears at bay now.

Nico manages to hide it until Rosie is on board.

Then he lets loose.

Seeing him swipe at his tears brings a fresh wave from me.

We both laugh at each other crying.

A few seconds later my cell phone rings. It's Rosalie.

"Hi," she says.

"Hi."

"We're in fancy seats."

"Of course you are," I say. "You're with your aunt Eva."

"We could make a bed from our seat."

"Cool. That's called first class."

She giggles. "I like it."

"Yep. It's not too shabby, is it?"

She is quiet for a second. "I'm going to miss you, Gia."

"I'm going to miss you, too," I say. "But I'll see you in three months. It's pretty much the same amount of time we'd be separated as when you used to go visit your dad."

"Yeah," she says, not sounding convinced.

"Here, talk to your dad," I say and hand him the phone.

Then he says goodbye.

"She said they are about to leave and asked her to shut off her phone."

"Oh."

We sit there for a few seconds in silence.

Then without a word, we both walk toward the floor-to-ceiling windows.

We stand in the window as the plane backs out and heads toward the runway.

Then we walk along the row of windows watching the plane. It ambles along for a while and then stops, lined up behind some other planes, waiting its turn. One by one the planes in front of it take off.

And then it is Rosalie's plane's turn.

It speeds down the runway, accelerating rapidly. We walk along the row of windows so we can keep it within our sight. It goes faster and faster. We walk faster and faster. Then, it lifts off the ground and is in the air. It arches higher and higher and still we walk and watch, peering out the windows until there are no more windows. We stand at the last window and watch.

And the plane grows smaller and smaller until it is hard to see.

And still we stand and stare at the tiny silver speck that contains our whole world until it disappears into the white sky.

And only then do we turn and head home.

The story continues in *Dark Shadows*, the next Gia Santella Thriller. Head to the next page for a sneak peek or scan the QR code below to order today!

Stay up to date with Kristi Belcamino's new releases by scanning the QR code below!
(You'll receive a **free** copy of *First Vengeance: A Gia Santella Prequel!*)

Did you enjoy *Cold Blooded*? Scan the QR code below to let us know your thoughts!

DARK SHADOWS CHAPTER ONE

When Nico and I first looked at apartments in Barcelona, we didn't have strong ideas about what we wanted other than it be located in the Gothic Quarter. The quarter was central to everything. It was near the beach and the main pedestrian artery of the city, Las Ramblas, and it overflowed with character. Below our balcony, the narrow street was filled with small mom-and-pop shops that had everything we could possibly desire—cheese, wine, bread. You know, the basic necessities.

But when we walked into this apartment, besides its gorgeous architecture, what I fell in love with was the alcove that was specifically designated as an ofrenda—a home altar for those you loved who had died. Even though I'm Italian and it's a Mexican tradition, it spoke to me on the deepest level of my soul.

Although some people only set up ofrendas around Dia de los Muertos, mine was in place all year long.

Now, as I wheeled my gunmetal gray suitcase over to the front door, I glanced at the altar. I would miss it the most. I wasn't sure when I'd be back in Barcelona. If ever.

The ofrenda was set in a deep oval alcove in the wall that contained photos, candles, and mementos from those I'd loved the most in this life: my parents, Bobby—my first true love, and Nico—my last true love.

Nico wasn't dead, but his picture was there along with all the other people I'd loved and lost in my life.

Was that sacrilegious? Fuck if I knew.

But the truth was the Nico I'd known and loved was dead.

Alzheimer's had taken him from me. He didn't know me anymore. Now, I was just some girl he groped when I showed up. At first it had broken my heart. But once I realized that the Nico I'd known and loved was no longer there, in some ways it'd been easier to let go.

I stared at the photos. The photo of my parents was one of them smiling on a boat, their hair windblown. My mother held a glass of wine. My father had his arm around her.

I missed my parents so much. I'd been robbed of them before I was barely old enough to drink. They had been my whole world.

The photo of Bobby was a snapshot I'd taken of him in Italy. He'd been standing on our balcony looking out at the sea. He was so damn handsome. That was the day I'd finally told him I loved him. Within 24 hours he'd be dead. The son of my parents' killer took him away.

A tear slipped down my cheek as I looked at the photo of Nico.

He looked like a sophisticated movie star and a powerful leader. Which is what he had been. My greatest love. The man I had intended to spend the rest of my life with. That man had loved me more than any woman could dream of being loved, but he had been taken away from me slowly and cruelly by the creeping dementia that stole his memories and light.

When I realized that Nico was gone, I decided to never allow myself to fall in love again.

It hurt too much. Why would I fucking torture myself like that again? Who in their right mind would do that? Um...nobody.

I was fucking done.

There is an old Italian saying that we only truly love three people in our lives.

I've loved my three.

Bobby. Nico. James.

Dear, sweet James who, thank God, was still alive and thriving in San Francisco. That man had stolen my heart but then broke it into a million pieces. Because I'm a killer and he was a cop. Our relationship never stood a chance.

I reached into my bag and took out my worn metal Zippo lighter and lit the candles on my ofrenda one last time.

I lit four of them. Along with the photos and candles, I'd placed mementos that reminded me of them or items that they had loved in life.

In front of Nico's picture, I'd placed a CD of his favorite music and a bottle of tequila.

For Bobby, a bottle of the hot sauce he loved and his favorite book of poetry.

For my parents, the cigars my dad liked and the perfume my mom wore.

My phone vibrated in my bag, startling me out of my memories.

I rummaged around and found it just as the call ended. Dante.

I called him back. "Yo."

"I've been buzzing. I'm downstairs."

"Oh, fuck. The ringer is still broken. I'll buzz you in."

I hit the button and headed back to the bedroom to finish packing my second suitcase.

Soon Dante was at my side.

"Have you decided where you're going?" he said in his perfectly enunciated speech as he walked in.

I glanced up at him and was once again astonished by his good looks. The guy never aged. We'd been friends since we were kids, and he just kept getting better looking. His brilliant white smile always stood out against his burnished olive skin, and I loved how he was wearing his silky black hair a little bit long in the back nowadays at the request of his husband, Wayne. Today, he was wearing a white linen shirt with the buttons undone enough for me to see his gold necklace with the Italian cornetto and hand talisman to protect against the evil eye.

"French Riviera," I said.

I continued throwing expensive silk lingerie into my smaller suitcase. Dante had made me buy it during our last shopping spree in Paris. I would never have spent $250 on underwear otherwise, but I had to admit it made my ass look spectacular.

"Sounds fabulous," Dante said, stepping into my closet. "Why there?"

"I have no memories there."

"What? That hurts. Me. You. St. Tropez?" he started humming some song about St. Tropez and dancing around.

"I'm not going there."

"Where to, then?"

I didn't answer, but I looked pointedly at a framed poster in the hallway. It was a still from the movie *La Piscine*. The movie was set in Italy. But from the look on Dante's face, I knew he made the connection. Cannes was the film epicenter of Southern France, and the festival was next week.

"Oh. My. God."

I hid my smile.

"What will you wear?"

"I'm going to sunbathe and read and listen to music and maybe find some hot boy to fuck."

Dante stopped dancing.

I could feel his disapproval without looking at him.

"You're married."

"Am I?"

He didn't answer.

I wasn't married. Not really.

How could I be? Nico didn't know who I was. He hadn't for months.

"At least let me dress you." Dante had personal buyers at all the top designers and attended the fashion shows in Paris every year. He had impeccable taste. Thank God one of us did.

"I'm bringing every bikini I own," I said. "That's really all I plan on needing."

"Darling, if you are going to be in Cannes during the Film Festival—first, how the holy hell did you find a place to stay there right now? Oh, never mind, you're Gia. But please, please tell me you'll let me dress you for the festival."

I shrugged and tossed another bikini into the suitcase on the bed.

"I wasn't planning on going to the festival."

"I'm going to get you tickets."

I didn't argue. I loved movies. Attending the festival in Cannes could fit into my hedonistic plans. "Sure. Whatever."

"Then it's a deal. Now, what should you wear? I'm not sure you have anything in this apartment?" He started thumbing through my hangers.

"I'll find something."

"I'll handle it," he said firmly. "Someone has to stop you from wearing your beat-up leather pants and 'Fuck Authority' T-shirt."

"Rosie took that shirt from me years ago."

Rosie was Nico's daughter. The closest thing I had to a child. She was off somewhere killing someone. Because, apparently, that's what the women in my family did. We couldn't help it. But there were always evil fuckers who needed to be killed.

"Will you let me do what I do best?" Dante said, in seventh heaven. Shopping and dressing me was his favorite thing ever. Or at least that's how it seemed.

"Yeah. I'll go watch some movies. And you can dress me for them."

Dante was chattering on and on about how he knew the perfect dress for me and that he might have to order it and have it sent to me in Cannes. But I would also need three other ones and...blah blah blah. I let him ramble. It made him happy so I tolerated it. And the simple fact was that I looked like shit when I dressed myself.

Attending the Cannes Film Festival was probably a legit reason to dress up.

Dante frowned. "There is nothing here. Nothing at all. Come with me," he said and grabbed my hand. "There is one place in town—one place in all of Barcelona—that might possibly have a dress that will do in a pinch if I can't get the dresses I have in mind ordered in time."

I couldn't help but laugh. God love Dante.

I grabbed my bag and followed him out the door, giving one last glance at the candles burning on the altar. I usually was very careful about blowing them out before I left the apartment, but I was feeling careless, reckless, and a small part of me thought that burning the place down would be apropos—leaving the charred remains of my life behind. But then I remembered other people lived in the building and leaned over to blow them out.

Then I steeled myself for some hard-core shopping. I wished I had some marijuana but would have to shop stone-cold sober.

But if I was being honest with myself, I was happy to spend another few hours with Dante.

He had flown into Barcelona from San Diego when he heard I was taking off for a few months...or forever.

It would be strange to leave Nico behind and not visit him daily while hoping there might be a glimmer of recognition in his eyes when he saw me.

There never was.

Nico was in good hands. I paid a small fortune every month for the memory care center to treat him like a king. It took about six months of him not recognizing me for me to realize my daily, doting presence there was no longer for him, only for me. And that it hurt like hell to be around him.

I was a coward.

I was going to leave him. Maybe forever.

If I thought there was the slightest, smallest part of him that still remembered me, I would stay. But there wasn't.

My heart was shattered.

Every morning I woke and lay in bed waiting for the dark shadows to recede from my nightmares only to realize that it wasn't a bad dream. It was my life.

Finally, I realized I had to leave Barcelona. At first I wanted to buy a house in the mountains somewhere and live like a recluse. There was still a chance I might. But right then, all my body craved was sunshine.

I'd spent the past few years as a caregiver, taking care of Nico, trying to glimpse fragments of who he used to be before he became angry and confused.

We rarely stepped outside unless it was to take him out to the garden for a walk. But now he refused to do even that.

I needed to lay in the sun and do things that weren't good for me so I didn't have to feel or think anymore.

Cannes would be the backdrop for my debauchery.

And I was happy to play it out there with all the other privileged fuckers who had everything that money could buy and yet wandered around hungrily trying to fill the empty void in their souls by spending recklessly, drinking too much, fucking everything with a heartbeat, and taking massive amounts of drugs.

DARK SHADOWS CHAPTER TWO

Nico was slouched in his leather lounger watching TV when I walked into his room.

He looked up at me, and for the smallest fraction of a second there seemed to be a glimmer of recognition in his eyes. Then he gave a wolfish smile.

"You my new nurse?"

I played along. "Do you want me to be?"

He shrugged. "I've seen worse."

I laughed out loud. It was that or cry.

He laughed too. But then he said, "I'm just giving you a hard time. You are a beautiful woman. When I was much younger I would've pursued you with everything I had."

I blinked back my tears. "I bet you were something else."

"Oh, boy, was I," he said and frowned. "At least that's what I've been told."

Even having a picture of me hugging him on the dresser in his room wasn't enough to jog his memory of our life together. He might look at it for a few seconds but would then ask why and where we had taken it.

But as hard as it was for me, Rose couldn't handle it at all.

She'd taken every picture of us as a family and herself out of his room.

I don't even know if she still came to visit him. She wouldn't answer when I asked.

She was in a dark place, and I couldn't reach her.

I called her on my way over to tell her I was leaving Barcelona for a while.

She didn't answer her phone so I left a message. Typical.

"What's on the agenda today?" Nico said, standing. I tried not to notice him reach out to grip the arm of the chair to steady himself. He was frowning.

"I thought we would take a walk in the garden," I said. "Get a little fresh air and sunshine."

"That's what you all say."

"That's because it's good for you."

He shuffled over to me. Along with the decline in his mental health, he had grown frail over the past few years. It was just another knife in my heart.

I wanted to help him, but I knew his ego couldn't handle it.

Outside, we walked for a while and then sat on a bench near a row of flowers.

He looked over at me., wringing his hands. At first it had bothered me, but the nurses told me it was common with Alzheimer's patients, and I'd gotten used to it. It was, like everything about Nico now, including the colostomy bag, so unlike the man I'd loved for so long.

"Do I know you?" he asked.

I smiled. "Yes."

"I mean before this?"

"What do you think?"

He stared at me hard. "I get really confused sometimes."

"It's okay," I said in the most comforting voice I could. Sometimes when I was with him and he was confused, he would grow angry and violent. It scared me. But I also didn't blame him. I was pissed off too.

Then he shook his head. He turned and stared straight ahead and said, "Maybe in another life."

"I think you're right. In another life."

"Do you believe in that?" he asked.

"Of course. Don't you?"

I'd never seen anything in my life as beautiful as his smile just then. "Yes. Yes, I do."

I looked away so he wouldn't see the tears falling down my cheeks.

Suddenly, he stood.

"I'm tired, nurse," he said. "I'm sorry I don't remember your name. I forget most things."

"I never told you my name. It's Gia."

He nodded. "That's a nice name."

"Thank you."

"Can you show me back to my room? I think I should take a nap."

"I'd be happy to do that, Mr. Morales."

I used his real name to see if he reacted. He didn't.

After I tucked him into bed and pulled the curtains in his room, I gave him a kiss on the cheek as I said goodbye. He acted surprised by the kiss, his forehead wrinkling up and his eyes squinting.

Of course he did.

But then he immediately seemed to forget it.

"Sleep well, Mr. Morales."

He didn't answer.

As I walked outside to the waiting car, I wondered if it was the last time I was going to see the man I'd considered my husband for so many years.

Are you loving *Dark Shadows?* Scan the QR code below to order your copy today!

ALSO BY KRISTI BELCAMINO

Enjoying Kristi Belcamino? Scan the code below to see her Amazon Author page!

Gia Santella Crime Thriller Series

Vendetta

Vigilante

Vengeance

Black Widow

Day of the Dead

Border Line

Night Fall

Stone Cold

Cold as Death

Cold Blooded

Dark Shadows

Dark Vengeance

Dark Justice

Deadly Justice

Deadly Lies

Additional books in series:

Taste of Vengeance

Lone Raven

Vigilante Crime Series

Blood & Roses

Blood & Fire

Blood & Bone

Blood & Tears

Queen of Spades Thrillers

Queen of Spades

The One-Eyed Jack

The Suicide King

The Ace of Clubs

The Joker

The Wild Card

High Stakes

Poker Face

Standalone Novels

Coming For You

Sanctuary City

The Girl in the River

Buried Secrets

Dead Wrong (Young Adult Mystery)

Gabriella Giovanni Mystery Series

Blessed are the Dead

Blessed are the Meek

Blessed are Those Who Weep

Blessed are Those Who Mourn

Blessed are the Peacemakers

Blessed are the Merciful

Nonfiction

Letters from a Serial Killer

ALSO BY WITHOUT WARRANT

More Thriller Series from Without Warrant Authors

Dana Gray Mysteries by C.J. Cross

Girl Left Behind

Girl on the Hill

Girl in the Grave

The Kenzie Gilmore Series by Biba Pearce

Afterburn

Dead Heat

Heatwave

Burnout

Deep Heat

Fever Pitch

Storm Surge (Coming Soon)

Willow Grace FBI Thrillers by Anya Mora

Shadow of Grace

Condition of Grace (Coming Soon)

Gia Santella Crime Thriller Series

by Kristi Belcamino

Vendetta

Vigilante

Vengeance

Black Widow

Day of the Dead

Border Line

Night Fall

Stone Cold

Cold as Death

Cold Blooded

Dark Shadows

Dark Vengeance

Dark Justice

Deadly Justice

Deadly Lies

Vigilante Crime Series by Kristi Belcamino

Blood & Roses

Blood & Fire

Blood & Bone

Blood & Tears

Queen of Spades Thrillers by Kristi Belcamino

Queen of Spades

The One-Eyed Jack

The Suicide King

The Ace of Clubs

The Joker

The Wild Card

High Stakes

Poker Face

AUTHOR'S NOTE

When I was 16, I read Jackie Collins' book, *Lucky*, and it rocked my world. For the first time in my prolific reading life (yes, I was the kid holed up in my room reading as many books as I could as often as I could), I met a character who was not only Italian-American like me, but a strong, powerful, and successful badass woman who didn't take crap from anybody and loved to have sex!

Although I had dreamed of being a writer, it never seemed like a realistic dream and my attempts at writing seemed pitiful. So I studied journalism and became a reporter—it was a way to be a writer and have a steady paycheck.

It was only when I was in my forties that I got the guts to write a book. And it was a few years after that I was brave enough to write the character I really wanted to write—Gia Santella.

She's not Lucky Santangelo, of course. I mean, nobody could be as cool as Lucky is, but I like to think that maybe Gia and Lucky would have been friends.

Gia is my alter ego. The woman who does and says things I

never could or would, but whom I admire and would love to be friends with.

If you like her, I'm pretty sure we'd be the best of friends in real life!

x Kristi

ABOUT THE AUTHOR

Kristi Belcamino is a USA Today bestseller, an Agatha, Anthony, Barry & Macavity finalist, and an Italian Mama who bakes a tasty biscotti.

Her books feature strong, kickass, independent women facing unspeakable evil in order to seek justice for those unable to do so themselves.

In her former life, as an award-winning crime reporter at newspapers in California, she flew over Big Sur in an FA-18 jet with the Blue Angels, raced a Dodge Viper at Laguna Seca, attended barbecues at the morgue, and conversed with serial killers.

During her decade covering crime, Belcamino wrote and reported about many high-profile cases including the Laci Peterson murder and Chandra Levy disappearance. She has appeared on *Inside Edition* and local television shows. She now writes fiction and works part-time as a reporter covering the police beat for the St. Paul *Pioneer Press*.

Her work has appeared in such prominent publications as *Salon*, the *Miami Herald*, *San Jose Mercury News,* and *Chicago Tribune*.

facebook.com/kristibelcaminowriter
instagram.com/kristibelcaminobooks
tiktok.com/@kristibelcaminobooks